Reader's House

available at

Editor's Picks

Betrayal

ALEATHA ROMING

"Wow! I was so looking forward to reading this, I love Aleatha's writing and Betrayal didn't disappoint!"

– Sarah T,

Paperback: £12.20

https://amzn.to/4fbN1pM

Faith

MIMI BARBOUR

"Was so glad to have Faith's story. Read first 4 books in the series and having Faith with her own happy ending, after all she had been through, was icing on the cake."

– Fran Kershner

Kindle: £0.85

https://amzn.to/3YwVY7p

Beautiful and Terrible Things

S.M. STEVENS

a compelling literary novel with resonant themes and characters that stay with readers after the last page is turned.

– Readers' Favorite

Paperback: £22.46

https://amzn.to/46hTQ53

The Hidden Gospel of Thomas

WILLIAM G. DUFFY

"I found new dimensions of Spirituality in reading this book, which is dear to my heart."

– Margaret Earing,

Paperback £12.99

https://amzn.to/3SjkhSb

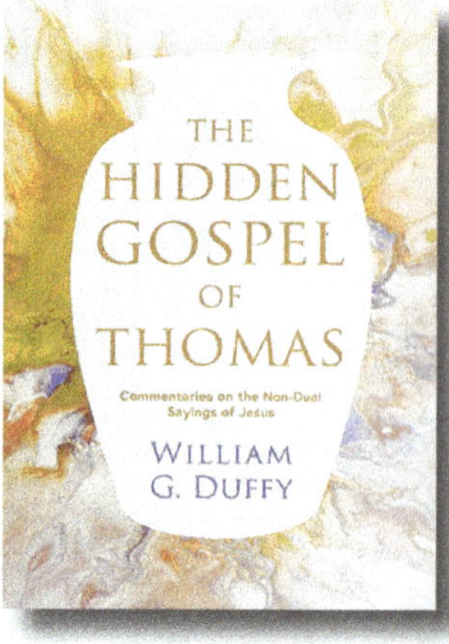

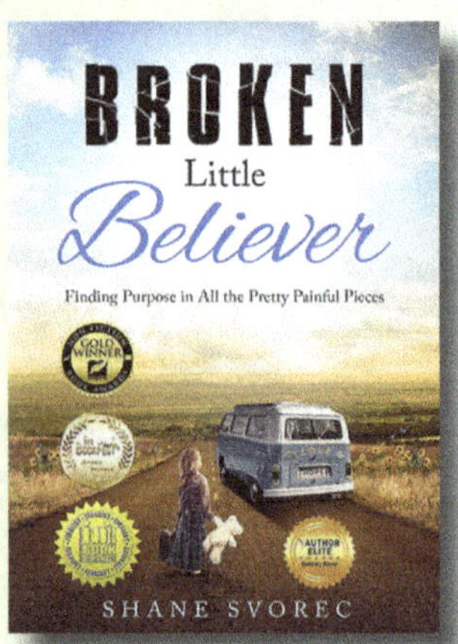

Broken Little Believer

SHANE SVOREC

"Wow, I could not put this book down! Shane is a talented writer and a beacon of light to all who have faced adversity and struggled to find their way. She gives each of us hope and inspiration that through faith, determination, and a positive attitude, there is a rainbow at the end of the storm. Wonderful book!"

–Barbara Kane, lifelong educator,

Hardcove: £12.43

https://amzn.to/4cPQTv7

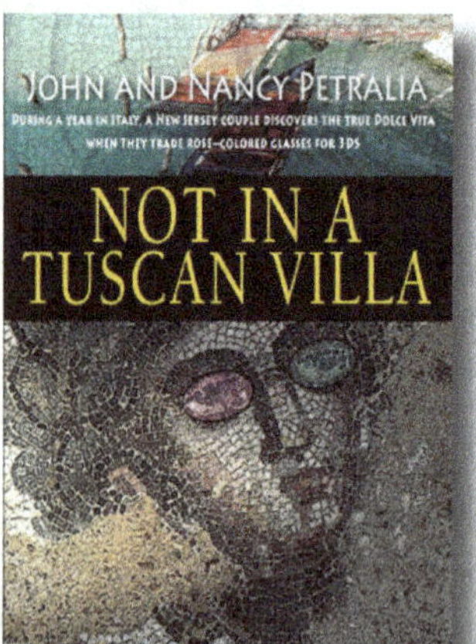

Not In a Tuscan VIlla

JOHN AND NANCY PETRALA

I so enjoyed this book that I read it straight through twice! A friend introduced me to it, and it is a very amusing account of a couples year living in Tuscany, but not at all sweet and cloying.

– Barbara Barrettt

Paperback: £11.14

https://amzn.to/4bVJ1GY

She Serves the Realm

LEE SWANSON

"A recommended read for those who like tales of strong women who defy stereotypes, beleaguered kings and nobles, and medieval England."

–J.P. Reedman, author of the Medieval Babes series

Paperback: £15.88

https://amzn.to/3A437By

Independence

CHRISTOPHER C TUBBS

Independence by Christopher C. Tubbs is a thrilling blend of naval warfare, espionage, and historical intrigue. A must-read masterpiece!

–Dan Peters, Reader's House,

paperback: £11.78

https://amzn.to/3zT3qPK

Your Gateway to Endless Stories

Escaping My Demons
JOSEPH FAGARAZZI

"Escaping My Demons is a hard-hitting, riveting, emotional memoir by Joseph Fagarazzi! The book focuses on the turbulent and tense relationships between Joseph and his parents, particularly his selfish, abusive, and exploitative father. "

– Steven Setil

Kindle: £7.95

https://amzn.to/3xZ4Mbg

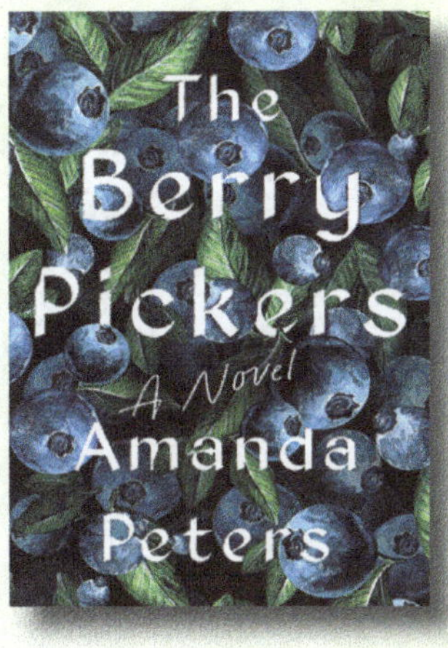

The Berry Pickers
AMANDA PETERS

"A gripping read, a mystery and a moving narrative all in one book."

– A New York Post Best Book of the Year

Paperback: £7.49

https://amzn.to/4bUk2DS

Thirteen Days in Milan
JACK ERICKSON

"The characters and plot in Jack Erickson' s *Thirteen Days in Milan* are alive, and the novel has enormous vitality. "

– Eduardo Elgani

Paperback: £8.40

https://amzn.to/4f7qD0V

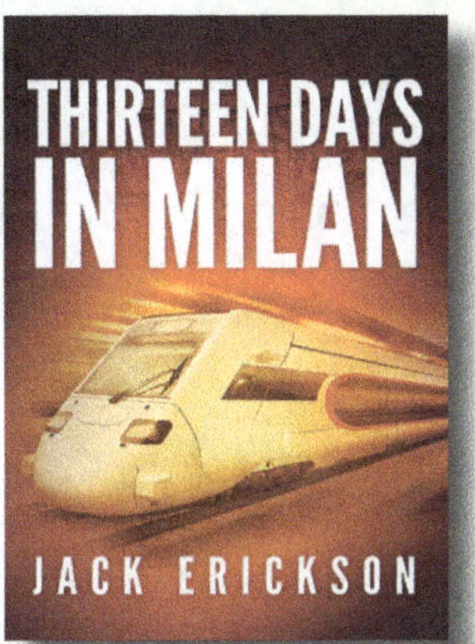

Run with It
JOE DRAKE

"You write beautifully, you've got both a sense of humor and a engineer's ability to make complex biological processes accessible to the non-scientist."

– Amazon Reviewer,

Hardcove: £19.54

https://amzn.to/3Lyt92n

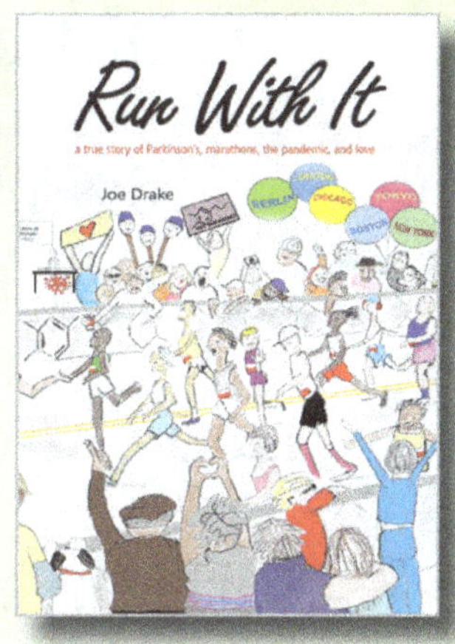

The Lost Bookshop
EVIE WOODS

"The story itself was fascinating. I loved all the details in the story.."

–Sandra A Harvey

Paperback: £8.99

https://amzn.to/3y8sdib

This is Why We Lied
KARIN SLAUGHTER

'Never less than nail-biting'
– The Times

Hardcover: £10.00

https://amzn.to/3zTe4pF

Savage Game
KAREN NAPPA

"About consent, but Karen Nappa, has usual found a way to play with dark desire, empowerment, seduction, and to create truly beautiful true consent. She is a master at this."

–Charnly M.

Paperback: £10.24

https://amzn.to/3WizHqW

A Paper Orchestra
MICHAEL JAMIN

"As one of the head writers for my tv show Maron, Michael Jamin was essential in helping me portray myself honestly. I'm very happy and impressed that he was able to apply his craft to himself..."

– Marc Maron

Hardcover: £20.73

https://amzn.to/3A1DuBn

IN THIS ISSUE

The Scribe's Symposium
A Journey into the Minds of Award-Winning Authors

8

ON THE COVER

Exploring the Spiritual Odyssey

ANN NAIMARK

A Touch of Light, Opening to the Love that is You and All Creation

Join Reader's House as Ann Naimark, a seasoned psychotherapist, shares insights on integrating spirituality into therapy, self-love, and personal growth in her enlightening interview.

SCAN TO READ
ONLINE

EDITOR'S LETTER

It is with immense pride and excitement that we present to you the 45th issue of Reader's House magazine, London's gateway to the literary world. This milestone issue is a testament to our unwavering commitment to bringing you the finest in literature, thought-provoking interviews, and inspiring stories from the world of books and beyond.

On our cover this month, we are honored to feature the exceptional Ann Naimark, a seasoned psychotherapist and spiritual guide whose journey of self-discovery and spiritual exploration is nothing short of transformative. In an exclusive interview, Naimark invites us into her world of profound insight and personal growth, sharing her unique approach to holistic wellness that seamlessly integrates the realms of body, mind, emotions, and spirit.

Naimark's story is one of evolution and enlightenment, from her early years as a skeptic to her transformation into a fervent advocate of spirituality. Her journey is a tapestry woven with threads of psychology, nursing, counseling, and spiritual exploration, making her a beacon of wisdom and compassion in the realm of psychotherapy. She shares pivotal moments that reshaped her worldview and ignited her quest for spiritual understanding, offering sage advice to those embarking on their own journey of self-discovery.

Central to Naimark's philosophy is the notion of self-love as a catalyst for spiritual growth and fulfillment. Through introspection, healing, and nurturing, she believes that one can cultivate a profound sense of self-compassion and acceptance, laying the foundation for spiritual awakening. Her practices, from daily rituals of gratitude to immersive experiences in nature, exemplify the art of harmonizing the diverse facets of existence.

As you delve into Naimark's illuminating book, *A Touch of Light*, you are invited to embark on a transformative odyssey of self-discovery and empowerment. With each page, she encourages readers to embrace their individuality, honor their unique paths, and seek out the sources of joy, peace, and fulfillment that resonate deep within their souls.

In addition to our cover story, this issue features interviews with a stellar lineup of award-winning authors, including John Shay,Eva Dietrich, Stanislava Buevich, Lara Gelya, Karl Muller, Lee Swanson, Stephanie Krol, Damien Dsoul, Marlena Frank, Terry Overton, Johan Cools, Michael A. Peck, Brad Balukjian, Marci Greenberg Cox, Tristan Zelden, Derek Borthwick, Christopher Link, Lynn Slaughter, Liz Alterman, Kelly E. Huston, Ashton August, Susan Mac Nicol. Each of these authors brings a unique voice and perspective to the literary landscape, and we are thrilled to share their insights and stories with you.

As we celebrate this milestone issue, we extend our heartfelt gratitude to you, our readers, for your continued support and enthusiasm. It is your passion for literature and the arts that fuels our mission to bring you the very best in literary content.

We hope that this issue of Reader's House magazine inspires you, enlightens you, and encourages you to embark on your own journey of self-discovery and spiritual exploration.

Happy reading!
A, Harlowe

PUBLISHER
Reader's House
A Subsidiary of Newyox Media
https://newyox.media

200 Suite
134-146 Curtain Road
EC2A 3AR London
t: +44 79 3847 8420

editor@readershouse.co.uk
readershouse.co.uk

EDITORIAL
A. Harlowe
editor@readershouse.co.uk
Dan Peters
dan.peters@readershouse.co.uk
Ben Alan
ben.alan@readershouse.co.uk

CONTRIBUTORS
Claudine D. Reyes
Acacia Baldie
Andrea Piacquadio
Adrian T. Cheng
Donna Schim
Jon Allo
Tim Halloran
Oleg Magni
Amir SeilSepour
Bill Youngblood
Jetty Stutzman
Jimmy Choo
Peter Filinovich
Rrodnae Productions

Reader's House

readershouse.co.uk

We assume no responsibility for unsolicited manuscripts or art materials provided from our contributors.

John Shay's Journey from Science to Storytelling
PANDA DEMICK
A Tale of Empathy and Environmental Awakening

John Shay, retired scientist, discusses inspiration behind "Panda Demick," weaving empathy, environmental themes amidst the pandemic. Collaboration with illustrator enriches narrative.

John Shay, a retired Earth scientist and high-tech entrepreneur residing in the vibrant city of Seattle, Washington, alongside his accomplished oceanographer wife, Joan, unveils a captivating narrative that intertwines the essence of familial joy with the global challenges of our time. With academic prowess steeped in chemistry and geophysics, Shay's journey spans groundbreaking achievements in the nascent era of streaming media to a tranquil retreat near the shores of Lake Washington, where he delves into a literary endeavour.

In the midst of a global pandemic that seized the world's attention, Shay welcomed the arrival of his grandson, a moment that juxtaposed the profound joy of familial bonds with the stark reality of a health crisis engulfing nations. It was within this juncture of personal bliss and societal upheaval that the seeds of inspiration for "Panda Demick" were sown. A tale not merely of a panda's adventures, but a poignant allegory reflecting our interconnectedness with nature, community, and the profound lessons gleaned from adversity.

Through the lens of Panda Demick's extraordinary ability to communicate with children, animals, and even the minutiae of viruses, Shay imparts a timeless message of empathy and resilience. Amidst the backdrop of a world in turmoil, readers are beckoned into a realm where compassion and understanding transcend boundaries, fostering a deeper appreciation for the delicate balance of our ecosystems.

Collaborating with the talented illustrator Jenny Zandona, Shay's narrative finds visual expression in a tapestry of illustrations that evoke the nuances of emotional transformation and environmental awakening. From the somber hues depicting ecological imbalance to the vibrant palette symbolizing renewal and hope, Zandona's artistry enriches Shay's storytelling, inviting readers of all ages to embark on a journey of self-discovery and collective renewal.

At its core, "Panda Demick" serves as a beacon of hope, resonating with readers young and old alike, navigating the tumultuous seas of life's challenges. Rooted in Shay's profound insights gleaned from a career bridging Earth science and entrepreneurship, the narrative transcends the confines of a mere children's tale, offering a poignant reflection on the urgent imperative of environmental stewardship and the enduring power of empathy in shaping a brighter tomorrow.

As Shay's magnum opus continues to captivate hearts and minds, "Panda Demick" stands as a testament to the indomitable spirit of human resilience, weaving together threads of compassion, friendship, and environmental consciousness in a tapestry of profound significance.

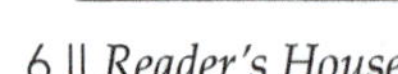

What inspired you to write Panda Demick, particularly during the COVID-19 pandemic?

I became a grandfather on March 13, 2020, three days after the World Health Organization declared COVID-19 a global pandemic. The stark juxtaposition of familial joy and global health threat got me thinking about my grandson's life and the world that he will be inheriting. It inspired me to write Panda Demick to provide caretakers a tool to help explain the pandemic in the context of the greater environmental crisis facing our planet. Panda Demick offers children insight into those complex issues in an uplifting and life-affirming manner.

The story is about a Panda, named Demick, who has the unique ability to talk to children, animals, and even itsy-bitsy viruses. His empathy and ability to listen to others provides him with the knowledge he needs to help his friends and others.

Can you tell us more about the message you aimed to convey through Panda Demick's adventures and friendships?

The one common experience we all had during the pandemic was the dramatic slowing of daily life. Instead of commuting into the office or school, we stayed close to home and reconnected with family members. As the roads and stores emptied our hearths and hearts filled up. We began to recall the importance of friendships and reconnecting deeply with our loved ones.

That slowing down of daily life is depicted in the story by illustrations of gathered family life during the pandemic as well as the calming of the animal kingdom as the world became quieter. Demick and his friends offer the reader an opportunity to imagine a world in better balance with nature.

Could you share a bit about your collaboration with illustrator Jenny Zandona? How did the illustrations complement your storytelling?

Jenny is a very talented children's book illustrator who is like a daughter to me. She was the first person I called when I decided to write the book. Her beautiful illustrations show the sadness of the environmental imbalance that preceded the arrival of the Coronavirus. Then, as the story unfolds, the experience of helping others during a time of crisis changes Demick, transforming him from a worrisome panda into a more confident and joyful panda. Demick's internal transformation is skillfully illustrated by a subtle color palette change that eventually results in our hero bursting into glorious color. His deep love for his friends and nature becomes visible to everyone.

Panda Demick seems to emphasise the importance of empathy and helping others in need. How do you believe this message can resonate with both children and adults, especially in challenging times like a pandemic?

One of my favorite illustrations in the book shows a nurse helping a masked elderly patient in a wheel chair. Resting on the floor next to them is an empty pair of nurse shoes. Those empty shoes represent the front-line healthcare workers we lost to the pandemic. That single image illustrates the best and worst of what we experienced during the pandemic. Children see the empathy of the nurse helping an elderly patient while an adult may recall the suffered losses and be able to offer insight to a child.

To help facilitate conversations with children about the pandemic, over 200 copies of Panda Demick have been gifted to front-line healthcare workers. The response from those healthcare works has been very positive.

How did your background in Earth science and high tech entrepreneurship influence the themes or ideas explored in the book?

From the beginning, I knew that the story of Panda Demick needed to be bigger than the Coronavirus. It needed to offer insight into how a tiny part of nature emerged and how its sudden arrival was a reflection of an ongoing environmental crisis. That environmental context for the story is tied directly to my early career as an Earth scientist. I hold degrees in both chemistry and geophysics. My first job out of college was working for The Greenhouse Gas Project at Scripps Institution of Oceanography in La Jolla, California. It was while working at Scripps that I met my wife, Joan, who holds a doctorate degree in oceanography. Together, we have had a front row seat to the hard-fact science behind climate change and its impact on ecosystems worldwide for over 45 years.

Journey into the Heart of Storytelling
An Interview with Eva Dietrich

Eva Dietrich, acclaimed author of The Giant Rainbow Hug, shares her inspiration and narrative philosophy in an exclusive interview with Reader's House, revealing the timeless magic of storytelling for children.

In the enchanting world of children's literature, where stories serve as bridges between imagination and reality, we often find gems that not only entertain but also nurture young minds with invaluable lessons. Eva Dietrich, the creative force behind "The Great Rainbow Hug," exemplifies this fusion of storytelling magic and meaningful narratives.

Dietrich, a distinguished author celebrated for her literary contributions, graciously shares her insights in an exclusive interview with Reader's House magazine. With a background enriched by Masters' Degrees in Children's Literature from the University of Surrey, London, and Creative Writing from the Metropolitan University of Manchester, UK, Dietrich is a luminary in the realm of storytelling. Moreover, as the founder and director of Aladdin Books & Media Agency, she continues to shape the landscape of children's literature.

Dietrich's multicultural upbringing, blending Spanish and German heritage, adds depth and richness to her storytelling palette. Currently residing in Madrid with her three children, alongside a vibrant menagerie of pets, Dietrich's experiences infuse her work with warmth, diversity, and a universal appeal.

The Great Rainbow Hug stands as a testament to Dietrich's narrative prowess, having been recognized by La Revue Des Livres Pour Enfants in 2011 as their annual selection. The heartwarming tale revolves around the endearing friendship between Sheiboob and Zipang, two unlikely companions who embark on a journey of discovery, love, and resilience.

In our interview, Dietrich delves into the genesis of her characters, shedding light on the inspiration behind Sheiboob and Zipang's unique bond. From the inception of these beloved characters as a monkey and a gorilla toy, to their profound friendship rooted in acceptance and courage, Dietrich unveils the layers of her storytelling craft.

Central to The Giant Rainbow Hug is the symbolism of a rainbow jumper, a poignant gift that transcends distance and embodies the essence of love and connection. Dietrich eloquently shares her creative process, illustrating how simple yet profound elements can resonate deeply with young readers, imparting invaluable life lessons.

Throughout the interview, Dietrich's passion for crafting relatable characters and narratives brimming with empathy shines through. Drawing from her own experiences as a mother and storyteller, she underscores the importance of nurturing emotional intelligence and fostering empathy through literature.

As children's literature continues to evolve, authors like Eva Dietrich serve as beacons of inspiration, weaving tales that not only captivate young hearts but also sow the seeds of kindness, resilience, and understanding. Join us as we embark on a journey into the enchanting world of "The Great Rainbow Hug," where every page is imbued with the magic of friendship, love, and the enduring power of storytelling.

Can you share more insights into the inspiration behind the characters of Sheiboob and Zipang and their unique bond in the story?

Initially, Sheibook and Zipang were a monkey and a gorilla toy. The uniqueness of their friendship lies in their ability to embrace their differences while having the courage to step out of their respective comfort zones and educate each other, all the while basking in the comfort of knowing they have each other's backs no matter what.

What message or theme were you aiming to convey through the relationship between Sheiboob and Zipang?

The main message I wanted to convey was that true friendship and love can withstand a little separation, can even be born in spite of physical separation, and that we will always carry the people who have touched our hearts with us wherever we go.

How did you come up with the idea of using a rainbow jumper as a significant gift in the story?

A warm, cosy jumper can easily be associated with a warm hug. If the jumper still carries the scent of a loved one, it can come very close to a warm, comforting hug. I think this is an image that young children can easily relate to.

A colourful rainbow is a symbol of hope, of the sun coming out after a storm, which can be associated with a soon-to-come reunion with a loved one, conveying the message that the separation is only temporary.

What motivated you to include elements of loneliness, friendship,

"Enter the enchanting world of The Giant Rainbow Hug,' where love knows no bounds and friendship bridges the gap between hearts."

and comfort in the narrative?

Every child experiences the fear and anxiety of separation from a parent, a close relative such as a grandmother, or even a friend, sibling or cousin. Loneliness, friendship and comfort are present from early childhood and throughout our adult lives. It is important for children to understand that they are not alone with these feelings and that there are ways to compensate for temporary feelings of loneliness, while also understanding that feeling lonely and being alone are not the same thing.

How do you approach creating relatable and engaging characters for children in your stories?

Staying connected to one's inner child is certainly one way to approach it. Having children of my own has given it a whole new meaning and perspective.

What do you believe is the importance of including valuable life lessons or morals in children's books?

Reading is an essential part of a child's emotional development and growth. It increases their empathy and compassion, as well as their understanding of the world around them and their role in it.

PHOTO: Eva Dietrich: Crafting Heartfelt Tales of Friendship, Love, and Resilience in 'The Giant Rainbow Hug'

ANN NAIMARK

A Touch of Light, Opening to the Love that is You and All Creation

Embark on a transformative journey of self-discovery and spiritual enlightenment with 'A Touch of Light' by Ann Naimark – a beacon of wisdom and compassion

BY BEN ALAN

In the pursuit of understanding ourselves and our place in the universe, the journey of self-discovery often takes unexpected turns, leading us toward realms of spirituality and introspection. Ann Naimark, a seasoned psychotherapist and spiritual guide, invites us into her world of profound insight and personal growth in an exclusive interview with Reader's House

Join Reader's House as Ann Naimark, a seasoned psychotherapist, shares insights on integrating spirituality into therapy, self-love, and personal growth in her enlightening interview.

magazine.

With a background rich in diverse experiences, Naimark's journey is a tapestry woven with threads of psychology, nursing, counselling, and spiritual exploration. Her re-lentless pursuit of holistic wellness, blending the realms of body, mind, emotions, and spirit, has shaped her into a beacon of wisdom and compassion in the realm of psychotherapy.

From her early years as a skeptic to her transformation into a fervent advocate of spirituality, Naimark's story is one of evolution and enlightenment. She shares pivotal moments that reshaped her worldview, igniting a quest for spiritual understanding that continues to unfold with each passing day.

Integral to Naimark's approach is the seamless integration of spirituality into her therapeutic practice. Recognizing the profound yearning for spiritual fulfilment among her clients, she emphasizes the importance of addressing the spiritual dimension alongside the psychological and emotional realms.

In this enlightening conversation, Naimark offers sage advice to those embarking on their own journey of self-discovery and spiritual exploration. She champions the uniqueness of individual paths, urging readers to heed the whispers of their hearts and find solace in communities of like-minded souls.

Central to Naimark's philosophy is the notion of self-love as a catalyst for spiritual growth and fulfilment. Through introspection, healing, and nurturing, she believes that one can cultivate a profound sense of self-compassion and acceptance, laying the foundation for spiritual awakening.

Balancing the multifaceted aspects of life – mental, emotional, physical, and spiritual – Naimark exemplifies the art of harmonizing the diverse facets of existence.

From daily rituals of gratitude to immersive experiences in nature, she shares practices that have been instrumental in her own spiritual journey.

As readers delve into Naimark's illuminating book, A Touch of Light, they are invited to embark on a transformative odyssey of self-discovery and empowerment. With each page, she encourages readers to embrace their individuality, honour their unique paths, and seek out the sources of joy, peace, and fulfilment that resonate deep within their souls.

In a world where spiritual awakening is both a personal quest and a collective endeavour, Ann Naimark

Continued *on page 10*

"Ann Naimark, psychotherapist and spiritual guide, illuminating paths to self-discovery and holistic wellness in her enlightening interview with Reader's House magazine.

emerges as a guiding light, offering insights and inspiration to all who seek to illuminate their path toward spiritual enlightenment.

What inspired you to write *A Touch of Light* and share your spiritual journey with

Ann Naimark's profound wisdom and compassionate guidance illuminate the path to self-discovery and spiritual growth. A truly enlightening interview!

readers?

When I was 30 years old, my dad (a prolific writer) suggested I write the story of my life. I listened, but couldn't imagine why anyone would want to read it?

Many years later I was having lunch in San Francisco with Ron, a 40-year friend. He wanted to write his life story. I recalled my dad's words. I had been feeling urges to do that too. As we talked, it felt like the shape of our books began to form. We agreed to support each other using his nun-teacher's advice, "If you want to write just AIC – get your ass in the chair!" So we began, checking in with each other- "have you AIC?"

Can you describe a pivotal

moment in your life that significantly influenced your perspective on spirituality?

I was raised an atheist. At 15 years old, one afternoon I was sitting outside in our backyard. A question appeared within, "Did my parents know all there was to know about spirituality?" I wanted to know. After college I began to explore different versions of spirituality.

How do you integrate spirituality into your work as a psychotherapist?

In my psychotherapy practice, I discovered that many clients wanted to talk about their spirituality. To meet their needs, I began asking them about the subject. I had felt from my 20's that we are physical, mental, emotional and spiritual and that we need to attend to all these parts in order to balance and become more whole as a person. I embraced this addition!

Now I ask as a matter of course. Many of my clients come work with me because I lead meditations and know meditative tools. Sometimes they want me to do that work with them.

What advice would you give to someone who is just beginning their journey of self-discovery and spiritual exploration?

Tune into what makes your heart sing! What do you love? Nature? Church? Singing? Praying? Yoga?

Be in community with like-minded folks who will support you and you, them. Explore. Read on spiritual subjects that interest you. Meditate with different groups to see how it feels to you. This is your journey, and it must fit your nature, your inclinations. It may change along the way. No matter. Go with your own flow. Tune into your feelings – does it feel right?

One way I know that something is good for me is when I get a calm feeling. Does the experience meet an emotional, mental, spiritual need?

In your experience, what role does self-love play in achieving spiritual fulfillment?

Self-love grows as you get to know yourself; you release your wound pain; you give yourself the benefit of the doubt. We all have some kind of emotional, mental, spiritual and/or physical pain.

This pain is there for a reason. It isn't because we are less than or flawed as a human in some way. I have found that all negative opinions, beliefs we have about ourselves, comes from some painful experience we've had, that we weren't helped to heal from. We carry these ideas, sometimes for years. Working with your inner child and helping that part of your psyche get what you needed those many years ago helps to grow compassion for yourself; helps self-love grow.

To me all of us is spiritual. When we attend to all aspects of ourselves we grow in self-love. When we find the spiritual focus that nurtures us and helps us to feel love from spiritual Sources, self-love grows even more.

My experience has been that when we hang out in Spiritual energy (to me, Source, Pure Love energy) we are automatically being cleaned up, like taking a shower or bath in Light. And the negative ideas, beliefs, etc. about ourselves begin to loosen up and release.

How do you balance the different aspects of your life—mental, emotional, physical, and spiritual?

I love to balance all of me. Waking up and being grateful for the day. Relating to nature – the trees, flowers, birds, animals. Talking to them and being grateful for them. Eating healthy for my body. Finding doctors that are on the same wavelength as I am. Exercising every day. Surrounding myself with people I love. Meditating every day.

I lead meditations and the people who come to those meditations nurture me.

All the above helps when I get thrown off course; when fear comes up. Talking to close friends I trust. Going to acupuncture, a chiropractor, getting a massage. Hearing live music or seeing a show. Anything that gives me breaks from the routine

Her books: thrilling, passionate, and unputdownable, weaving tales of love, suspense, and adventure that leave readers craving more.

of life that is fun for me.

Could you share some of the most impactful practices or techniques that have helped you on your spiritual journey?

EMDR (eye movement desensitization and restructuring) is very helpful. I've done it personally and I use it a lot with clients. Tapping (EFT) helps to balance all parts of us and release stress.

Hatha Yoga was one of the first techniques I learned in my 20's. I loved the deep relaxation at the conclusion of the practice where you are focused on your body and paying attention to every part; getting to know how each part feels.

What do you hope readers will take away from *A Touch of Light* after reading your book?

My goal for A Touch of Light is to encourage readers to pursue their own life path their own way. We are all different. We're drawn to different spiritual styles. What works for one won't work for another. Find what helps YOU emotionally, spiritually, mentally and physically. I am not a marathon runner, but some people love it and gets them into a meditative state where they feel joy and lightness. It feeds them. What feeds you and brings you joy, peace, freedom, balance, love?

ANN NAIMARK

Ann earned a BA in Psychology at Hobart and William Smith Colleges. Became an LVN and then an RN. Then received an MA in Counseling from the University of San Francisco. She has been working as a psychotherapist (Marriage and Family Therapist) since 1993 both in mental health agencies and her own private practice.

She began incorporating spirituality into her counseling work when clients said no one was talking about this subject in their lives. She has felt for many years that attending to and integrating body, mind, emotions, and spirit are all important to being a whole person and assisting a person in living a life of joy, peace and love.

In addition, she has led group meditations for many years and taught classes in various spiritual subjects.

Celebrating our human diversity, Ann adheres strongly to the idea that there are many ways to our spiritual evolution. She honors everyone's experience and inclination and supports each person in their unique style.

EDITOR'S NOTE

A Touch of Light is a transformative, inspiring guide to self-love and spiritual awakening, beautifully written and deeply resonant.

A Touch of Light by Ann Naimark is a heartfelt and transformative guide to discovering self-love and deeper spiritual connection. Naimark's personal narrative, set against the backdrop of a seemingly perfect suburban life, reveals a profound journey from inner turmoil to spiritual awakening. Her candid storytelling and relatable struggles make this book an inspiring read for anyone seeking greater peace, joy, and self-acceptance.

Naimark skillfully blends personal anecdotes with practical advice, offering readers actionable steps to release negative emotional patterns and embrace their true nature. The book's emphasis on living in day-to-day awareness of Source and trusting one's inner instincts resonates deeply, a roadmap to a more balanced and fulfilling life.

Each chapter serves as a beacon, guiding readers towards greater self-discovery and acceptance. Naimark's gentle encouragement to love one's sensitive nature and view life as an adventure is particularly empowering. Her insights into discerning divine guidance and moving closer to or dreams are both enlightening and practical.

REVIEW

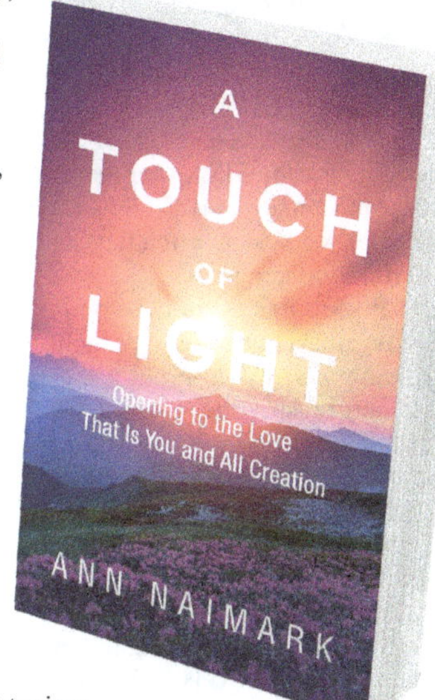

While the book's spiritual focus might not appeal to everyone, those open to its message will find it a valuable companion on their journey to self-realization. A Touch of Light is a beautifully written testament to the transformative power of self-love and spiritual connection, leaving readers with a renewed sense of their own vibrant, joyful essence.

STANISLAVA BUEVICH

Unveiling the Journey of a Multifaceted Storyteller

Award-winning filmmaker Stacy Buevich discusses her transition to novel writing, inspirations for children's books, suspense novels, and upcoming detective series.

Stanislava Buevich is a creative force to be reckoned with, seamlessly blending the worlds of film and literature in ways that captivate and inspire. Known for her distinctive style that intertwines surrealism and quirkiness, Buevich has carved out a unique niche for herself. She is a British writer and acclaimed film director whose unique, genre-blending style has captivated audiences across multiple mediums. Born in Moscow, her journey has taken her across the globe—from the USA to Finland, Switzerland, and now the UK—imbuing her work with a rich tapestry of cultural influences.

Initially gaining acclaim as a film director, Buevich's repertoire includes numerous award-winning short films and music videos. However, it was during the global lockdown that she transitioned into the realm of novel writing, beginning with the enchanting "Maya Fairy," a magical mystery inspired by her daughter. This marked the start of a prolific writing career that now boasts several novels, including the upper middle grade horror tale "Clearlake," which draws deeply from her personal experiences.

Buevich's academic background is as diverse as her professional one. She holds a degree in Psychology from University College London and refined her filmmaking skills at the prestigious Met Film School in Ealing Studios. Currently based in Singapore, she is embarking on a new academic pursuit with a Master's Degree in Creative Writing at LASALLE University of the Arts. This new chapter promises to further enrich her storytelling capabilities as she continues to explore new avenues of creative expression.

With a new book, "The Soultrapper," on the horizon—a sci-fi young adult mystery and adventure—Buevich shows no signs of slowing down. She is also working on several adult fiction projects under the pen name Stacy Kay, highlighting her versatility and breadth as a writer. Her upcoming works promise to offer readers a blend of suspense, magic, and deeply personal narratives, all delivered with the unique flair that has become her hallmark.

In this interview, we delve into Buevich's multifaceted career, her transition from film to literature, and the inspirations behind her compelling stories. Join us as we explore the mind of this extraordinary storyteller, whose passion for narrative is matched only by her drive to create and connect with audiences worldwide.

What inspired your transition from being a multi-award-winning British filmmaker and screenwriter to delving into the world of novel writing?

The short answer is COVID, but the long one is a bit more complicated. Before COVID, I was primarily directing short films and music videos for up-and-coming artists. I always wanted to write and direct feature films, but having no connections in the industry and being an introvert, I found it extremely difficult to get my projects off the ground. "Geoffrey's Heart" was meant to be my debut feature film. I had the script ready and was collaborating with a producer. When COVID hit, everything collapsed. Suddenly, I was stuck at home with my very energetic, now home-schooled, four-year-old daughter, thinking I would lose my mind unless I found a creative outlet. I started writing "Maya Fairy" for my daughter, but it turned out to be a book for me. It was an inexistent genre meant to bridge the gap between children's literature and women's fiction. Obviously, the book wasn't a huge success. However, holding the finished product in my hands, I realized just that - it was finished. I had made something precious for my daughter, and unlike "Geoffrey's Heart," I held something tangible, something whole and complete, something I could be proud of. From that moment on, I couldn't stop writing.

Can you share some of the key themes and inspirations behind the children's books you've penned, and what motivated you to craft stories specifically for young readers?

As I already mentioned, my daughter Maya was my main motivation. I wanted to write something for and about her, but also about us as a unit. Although "Maya Fairy" is still very much fiction, the emotions are all true. "Clearlake" was my second novel for kids, but I stepped up the age range. It's meant for an Upper Middle Grade audience. It is also deeply personal and fictionalises my relationship with my mother. It is a horror story, and much of it is made up, but a surprising amount is not. My third book for kids, which I am launching soon, is "The Soultrapper," a sci-fi YA mystery. From then on, most of my upcoming projects are for adults, which I will write under a different pen name - Stacy Kay (which is my nickname and married name). I do have a few more outlines for YA that I have yet to start writing. I have a diverse taste in film and literature and don't want to limit myself to just one genre or age range.

Your upcoming suspense novel sounds intriguing. Could you provide us with a glimpse into what readers can expect from this thrilling tale, and what inspired you

'Maya Fairy' by Stanislava Buevich, with illustrations by Diana Akhmetova, is a captivating tale that brings the magic of fairies to life. Buevich's storytelling is enchanting and engaging, making it a must-read for children and adults alike. A delightful blend of mystery and fantasy, beautifully illustrated.

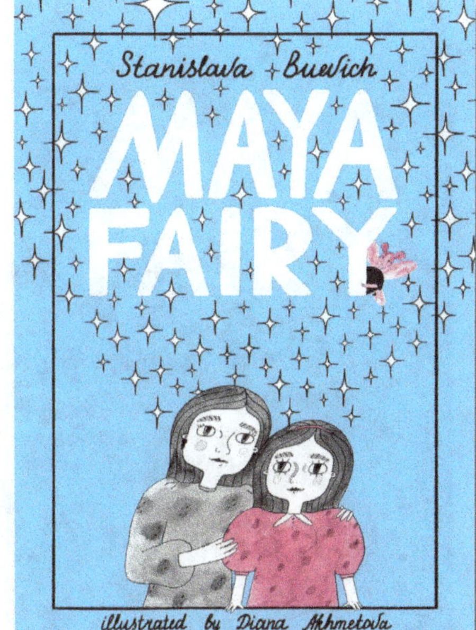

to explore the suspense genre?

I think all of the books I've written so far (except one, which is magical realism and political satire) have an element of suspense. What I write reflects my personal taste. Sometimes I think I should be more pragmatic and write for the market, but at the end of the day, I write books that I want to read. I have three books in different editing stages that fall under the suspense genre to varying degrees. "The Soultrapper" is a YA sci-fi mystery, "Alyona, Anna, Alisa" (working title) is an erotic thriller, and "Remember Bangkok" is a detective fiction novel, the first in a series.

You mentioned developing a new series of detective novels. What can readers anticipate from this series in terms of mystery, intrigue, and character development?

I was a huge fan of Agatha Christie growing up, and "Remember Bangkok" pays homage to her work. My detective, Jessica Tan, is a disheartened millennial who discovers her hidden talent for detective work when a guest at the hotel where she works dies mysteriously. I am currently based in Singapore, and this is my first book that is not set Europe. Jessica will travel across the world in the first and subsequent books, making it a real global adventure. I've been lucky enough to live in six different countries across three continents, and I'm a keen traveler. This series of books is greatly inspired by my experiences. I am halfway done with book one and have four more roughly outlined.

Your passion for magical realism and thrillers is evident. How do you infuse elements of magic and suspense into your storytelling, and what draws you to these particular genres?

My taste in films and literature inspires what I write. Most of my favorite books—One Hundred Years of Solitude, One Hundred Shadows, Slaughterhouse-Five, Master and Margarita—fall under the magical realism category. Most of my films are horror, although of the subtle, comedic, often magical kind. Because I read and watch a lot in this genre, it comes naturally to me to infuse my own work with the surreal.

As you embark on this literary journey, how do you plan to connect with your audience through your blog, newsletter, and other platforms?

Gosh, I really should up my game when it comes to this. I am writing (albeit very slowly) a prologue for "Clearlake," as a lot of readers wanted one. I will distribute it for free via my website (https://www.stacywritesbooks.com/), where you can also subscribe to my newsletter. I always promise myself to be more active on social media, @Stacywritesbooks on Instagram and TikTok, but truth be told, I'm a bit rubbish at that. However, I am always on Goodreads, and I often post reviews of the books I read. I'm starting a Master's degree in creative writing this year and planning to document my journey. Maybe that could make for an interesting blog?

Beyond Borders - Gelya's Path from Kyzylkum* to Award-Winning Author

LARA GELYA

A Life Shaped by Gladiolus Hues and Literary Legends

Author Lara Gelya, a literary voyager whose narratives reflect a kaleidoscope of life experiences, surrounded by the vivid hues reminiscent of the gladiolus blooms that colored her childhood memories.

In the colourful tapestry of the literary world, certain authors bring unique hues that stem from their extraordinary life experiences. Lara Gelya, an award-winning author, carries a narrative as vibrant as the myriad shades of the gladiolus flowers she fondly recalls from her childhood in Ukraine. Her journey spans continents, professions, and languages, weaving a tale that resonates with resilience, curiosity, and an unwavering love for storytelling.

Born amidst the landscapes of Ukraine, Lara's life traversed the expanse of the Kyzylkum Desert in Uzbekistan before finding a home in the United States. Her narrative, a testament to perseverance and reinvention, echoes the spirit of exploration ingrained in her through years spent amid geological expeditions and diverse cultural landscapes.

The beauty of Lara's literary odyssey lies not only in her award-winning book, "Camel from Kyzylkum," but in the rich tapestry of influences that shaped her as both a person and a writer. In her conversation with The Reader's House, Lara delves into her early love affair with books, paying homage to Russian literary giants like Pasternak and Chekhov, alongside American luminaries such as Hemingway and Poe.

Her journey into the English language mirrors a symphony, where the melody gradually unfolds over a decade, allowing her to discern the nuanced cadences that echo through different narratives. Gelya's penchant for historical fiction and classics, coupled with her appreciation for memoirs and personal development books, sheds light on the diverse reservoir of inspiration that fuels her creativity.

Amidst the interview's pages, Lara invites readers into cherished memories of her childhood, where the hues of gladiolus blossoms and the impactful narratives of early readings left indelible imprints on her soul. Her narrative encapsulates not just a literary journey, but a tapestry woven with sensitivity, trustworthiness, and an unyielding commitment to integrity—traits rooted in her character from the very beginning.

As Gelya candidly shares her challenges in penning her memoir in a language acquired later in life, she exemplifies the essence of perseverance and dedication that defines her work. Her admiration for fictional characters, particularly Claire Randall from "Outlander," offers a glimpse into her appreciation for resilient, independent spirits who refuse to be confined by societal norms.

In Lara Gelya's narrative, readers will discover more than an author—they will encounter a storyteller whose life experiences serve as both ink and parchment, etching tales of resilience, transformation, and a deep love for the written

word. Join us as we delve into the intricate world of Lara Gelya, a literary voyager whose narratives mirror the kaleidoscope of human experiences.

Born in Ukraine and going to school there, Lara Gelya went on for the next 20 years to the Kyzylkum Desert of the Republic of Uzbekistan, working at geological sites and expeditions of the Mining Industry. At that time Ukraine and Uzbekistan were parts of one country—the Soviet Union.

In 1989 Lara left the Soviet Union, lived in Austria and Italy before she, at last, found her way to the United States in 1990. Starting her life from ground zero again, and trying on so many hats, she was able to make a lengthy professional career that led to her eventual retirement on the shores of sunny Florida.

In September of 2022 Lara became an award-winning author as her book, Camel from Kyzylkum, was awarded with the Literary Titan Gold Book Award.

When she isn't writing or making her videos and pictures, Lara spends most of her time reading, gardening, cooking, traveling the world, wandering through nature, or catching her favourite shows.

What kind of reader were you as a child?

I have loved books from my very early years. Started by reading books by Korney Chukovsky, Samuil Marshak, Agniya Barto,

Olga Perovskaya, later Lev Kassil, Anton Chekhov, and many others.

Who are your favourite writers? Are there any who aren't as widely known as they should be, whom you'd recommend in particular?

Boris Pasternak, Konstantin Paustovsky, Ivan Turgenev, Anton Chekhov, Aleksandr Pushkin, to name a few, are among my favorites in Russian literature; Vladimir Nabokov, Russian-American novelist, poet, translator, whom I discovered after I came to the USA. Among American writers, my favorites are Jack London, Ernest Hemingway, Edgar Poe, Maya Angelou, and many more. Currently, I'm reading "A Land Remembered", a novel by Patrick D. Smith, the most outstanding Florida historical novel. I'm not sure if it is widely known, but I can definitely recommend it to readers who love historical novels.

What moves you most in a work of literature?

Language is always the living soul of a narrative, it is like a piece of music specific to the writer's voice. When I came to the USA in 1990, I did not know any English. It took me about 10 years before I really started to hear and feel the music of the language in different books and distinguish my likes and dislikes when reading books written in English.

What genres do you especially enjoy reading?

My favorites are historical fiction and classics. I also like memoirs, short stories, inspirational books, and non-fiction books about personal development.

What books and authors have impacted your writing career?

Writers are influenced by what they see, hear, and read. Most writers were and are avid readers. As a result, the works of other writers influence a writer. As I wrote a memoir of my life journey I just wanted to tell the World my untold story inside of me.

What is a childhood memory that makes you smile?

I was born in Ukraine in the city of Vinnitsa, which is southwest of Kiev, the capital of Ukraine. In my earlier years, I had a girlfriend, named Natasha. Natasha lived with her parents and a little sister across the street from us. Natasha and I played together. Her father was a teacher at the university and in his free time he liked to grow gladiolus flowers in his little yard. Every time I was visiting them during the summer days, he proudly showed me his little garden, explaining all the interesting characteristics of different types of gladiolus plants. Even now I can close my eyes and picture his little garden with a rainbow of gorgeous colors, ranging from white, yellow, pink and lavender, to rose, burgundy, purple, and even black. My love to have flowers around my house comes from that time of my childhood.

Do you remember the first story you ever read and the impact it had on you?

The greatest impact on me in my earlier years was from the novel "Wild Dog Dingo or the Tale of the First Love" written by Ruvim Frayerman. This book and the film shot in 1962 (in the Soviet Union), are still among my favorites.

As you grew older, what are the most important traits from your childhood that you held onto?

I think my personality is characterized by a focus on internal feelings rather than on external sources of stimulation. I'm a very sensitive person. Trustworthiness, honesty, integrity, and loyalty always were and still are very important traits for me.

What attributes make one a great writer?

Attention to detail. Great writers are observers, always taking men-tal notes and noting subtle changes around them.

What challenges did you face while writing your first memoir?

English is my second language. I started to learn it when I was 40 years old and I am still learning it every day. I think everyone can imagine that it was not easy for me to write a book in English.

If you had the power to bring any fictional character from any book or movie or TV series to life, who would it be and why?

Claire Randall/Fraser from Outlander, played by Caitriona Mary Balfe, an Irish actress, producer, and former fashion model. Claire is independent, headstrong, and cool under pressure. She doesn't take orders well, and she doesn't keep quiet. And I love how Jamie calls her with a term of endearment: Sassenach. It means a foreigner. And more specifically, it's a less-than-kind Gaelic word for an English person. But Clair has no idea that it's a derogatory term, she knows Jamie's plainly not trying to insult her. He's just pointing out that she's strange. After we watched "Outlander", my husband calls me Sassenach too.

*Kyzylkum is a large desert region in Central Asia, spanning across Kazakhstan, Uzbekistan, and Turkmenistan. The name "Kyzylkum" translates to "Red Sand" in Turkic languages, describing the reddish tint of the sand found in this desert. It's one of the largest deserts in the region, characterized by its arid landscape and nomadic settlements.

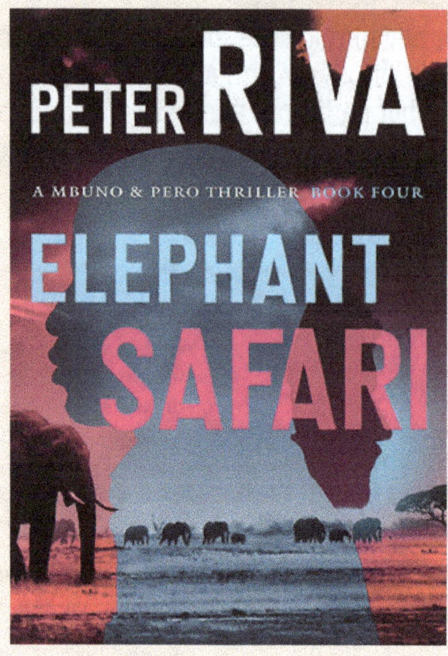

JUST SAY IT

by Tessa Barrie

"Just Say It by Tessa Barrie is a beautifully written, insightful family drama that masterfully explores love, forgiveness, and personal growth.

Just Say It by Tessa Barrie is a poignant family drama that delves into the complexities of unconditional love and personal growth. The story follows Lisa Grant, who, at forty, is broke, alone, and facing a midlife crisis in rural Gloucestershire. Her inability to express love has estranged her from Jack, the love of her life, now living in New York.

Central to Lisa's turmoil is her relationship with her narcissistic mother, Elizabeth. The mystery of her father's disappearance when she was six and Elizabeth's secrecy about it haunts Lisa. As a journalist, Lisa reconnects with her father and uncovers unsettling truths about her mother.

Determined to understand Elizabeth's lack of empathy, Lisa investigates her mother's past, revealing childhood traumas that reshape her perspective. Barrie skillfully portrays the complexities of familial relationships, capturing the pain, frustration, and moments of tenderness that define them.

Just Say It is a beautifully written novel that resonates with anyone who has grappled with difficult family dynamics or sought to make peace with their past. Tessa Barrie's storytelling is engaging and insightful, making this book a must-read for fans of family dramas.

ELEPHANT SAFARI

by Peter Riva

Elephant Safari is a gripping, fast-paced adventure with vivid descriptions and well-developed characters, raising crucial wildlife conservation awareness.

Elephant Safari by Peter Riva is a thrilling and immersive adventure that takes readers deep into the heart of East Africa. This gripping tale follows documentary producer Pero Baltazar, his camerawoman Nancy Breiton, and their elite guide Mbuno Waliangulu as they embark on a walking safari to reconnect with the wildlife they cherish. However, their peaceful journey quickly spirals into a chaotic and dangerous mission to protect a herd of migrating elephants from ruthless poachers.

Riva's storytelling is both vivid and engaging, painting a rich tapestry of the African landscape and its diverse wildlife. The author's deep knowledge of the region and its complexities shines through, making the setting come alive for readers. The plot is fast-paced and filled with suspense, keeping you on the edge of your seat as Pero and his team navigate the treacherous terrain and face off against a network of poachers whose reach extends far beyond the African bush.

While the book is a thrilling read, it also serves as a poignant reminder of the urgent need for wildlife conservation. The author's passion for the subject matter is evident, and readers will find themselves both entertained and enlightened by the narrative.

Elephant Safari is a must-read for fans of adventure and wildlife conservation. Peter Riva has crafted a compelling story that not only entertains but also raises awareness about the critical issues facing endangered species. With its well-drawn characters, breathtaking setting, and high-stakes plot, this book is a standout addition to the Mbuno & Pero Thrillers series.

ARESTI

by Evelyn Dunbar Webb

Aresti: Planet of the Red God is a thrilling, immersive adventure with rich world-building and compelling characters. Highly recommended!

Evelyn Dunbar Webb's "Aresti: Planet of the Red God Volume I: Foothills of the Gods" is a captivating entry into the realm of young adult science fiction and fantasy. The story follows sixteen-year-old Blaas Rakendo, known as Rake, who is brash, impatient, and believes he has all the answers. Armed with his grandfather's journals and a handful of relics, Rake embarks on a journey to solve the puzzle of his inheritance, only to find himself entangled in a web of political intrigue and dark secrets.

Webb's world-building is rich and immersive, drawing readers into the mysterious and complex world of ArestI. The narrative is well-paced, with a perfect blend of action, mystery, and character development. Rake is a compelling protagonist whose journey from a headstrong teenager to a more mature individual is both believable and engaging.

The plot is filled with twists and turns, keeping readers on the edge of their seats. The political intrigue and the dark secrets that Rake uncovers add depth to the story, making it more than just a simple adventure tale. The supporting characters are well-developed, each adding their own unique flavor to the story.

One of the standout aspects of the book is Webb's ability to create a sense of urgency and danger. The threats that Rake faces are real and immediate, and the stakes are high. This makes for a thrilling read that is hard to put down.

Aresti is a must-read for fans of young adult science fiction and fantasy. Evelyn Dunbar Webb has crafted a compelling and immersive story that will leave readers eagerly awaiting the next installment.

EDITOR'S CHOICE

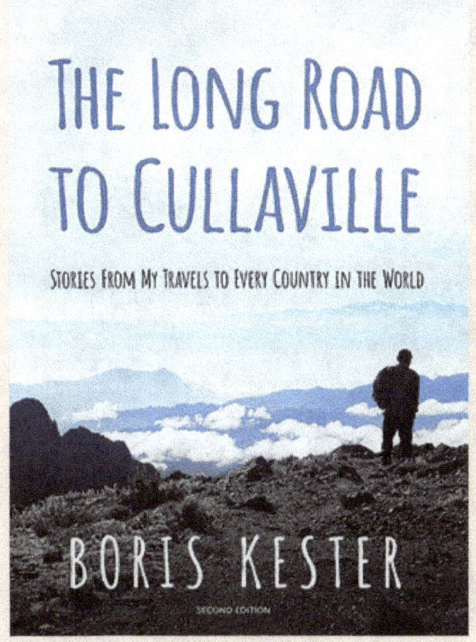

AL:ICE
by CW Lamb

BLOOD INHERITANCE NOVELS
by M. Ainihi

THE LONG ROAD TO CULLAVILLE
by Boris Kester

AL:ICE by C.V. Lamb is a captivating sci-fi adventure with a compelling protagonist, thrilling plot twists, and immersive world-building. Highly recommended!

AL:ICE by C.V. Lamb is a thrilling and imaginative science fiction novel that captivates readers from the very first page. The story follows Captain Jacob Thomas, a divorced combat veteran, who finds himself entangled in a high-stakes mission involving advanced artificial intelligence and interstellar intrigue.

Lamb's writing is both engaging and thought-provoking, seamlessly blending action with deep philosophical questions about humanity and technology. The characters are well-developed, with Jacob Thomas standing out as a particularly compelling protagonist whose personal struggles add depth to the narrative.

The plot is fast-paced and filled with unexpected twists, keeping readers on the edge of their seats. The world-building is detailed and immersive, making the futuristic setting feel both believable and fascinating.

Overall, *AL:ICE* is a must-read for fans of science fiction. C.V. Lamb has crafted a masterful tale that is both entertaining and intellectually

.

The Blood Inheritance Novels Two-Book Set is a captivating fantasy series with rich characters, immersive world-building, and an enthralling plot.

The *Blood Inheritance Novels Two-Book Set* is a remarkable journey into a world filled with magic, intrigue, and complex characters. This set, which includes "Endow" and "Resist," offers readers a seamless blend of fantasy and adventure that keeps you hooked from the first page to the last.

The storyline is well-crafted, with a perfect balance of action, suspense, and emotional depth. Each book builds upon the other, creating a cohesive narrative that is both engaging and thought-provoking. The pacing is excellent, ensuring that there is never a dull moment.

The characters are richly developed, each with their own unique backstories and motivations. The protagonists are relatable and their growth throughout the series is both believable and inspiring. The supporting characters add depth to the story, making the world feel lived-in and real.

The world-building in this series is exceptional. The author has created a vivid and immersive world that is easy to get lost in. The descriptions are detailed without being overwhelming, allowing readers to visualize the settings and understand the rules of the world effortlessly.

The writing is fluid and engaging, with a perfect blend of dialogue and narrative. The author's style is accessible yet sophisticated, making it suitable for both young adults and older readers.

The set is a must-read for fans of fantasy and adventure. It offers a compelling story, memorable characters, and a richly detailed world. Whether you are a long-time fan of the genre or new to it, this series is sure to captivate and entertain.

Boris Kester's 'The Long Road to Cullaville' is a captivating, inspiring travel memoir that vividly brings global adventures to life.

Are you ready to explore the world's most intriguing destinations? Boris Kester's *The Long Road to Cullaville* is a captivating and inspiring travel memoir that takes readers on an extraordinary journey to every corner of the globe. With a perfect blend of adventure, culture, and personal anecdotes, this book is a must-read for both seasoned travelers and those who dream of exploring the world from the comfort of their armchair.

Boris Kester, a man of many talents—senior purser, programmer, political scientist, sports enthusiast, polyglot, and fearless adventurer—embarks on an audacious mission to visit every country in the world. His passion for travel and exploration is evident in every page, as he vividly describes the breathtaking landscapes, vibrant cultures, and memorable encounters he experiences along the way.

The book is a collection of sixteen enthralling stories, each one an open invitation to immerse yourself in the magic of travel. Kester's vivid descriptions and keen observations bring each place to life, making it easy to visualize the stunning scenery and feel the pulse of the local culture. His encounters with people from all walks of life add depth and richness to the narrative, highlighting the universal connections that bind us all.

The book is more than just a travel memoir; it is an inspiring testament to the power of wanderlust and the transformative impact of exploring the unknown. Whether you are a seasoned globetrotter or someone who dreams of far-off places, this book will ignite your curiosity and inspire you to see the world in a new light.

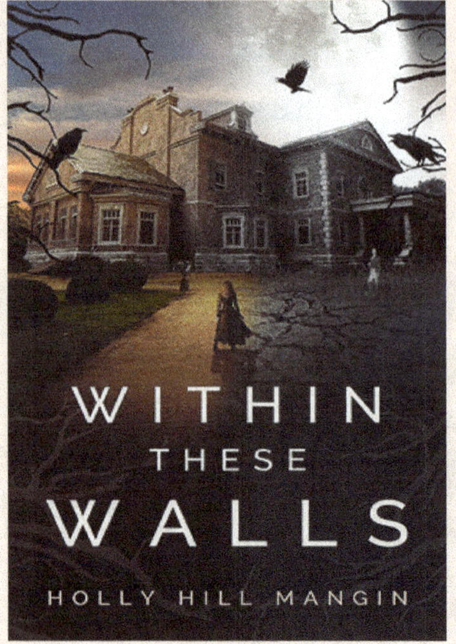

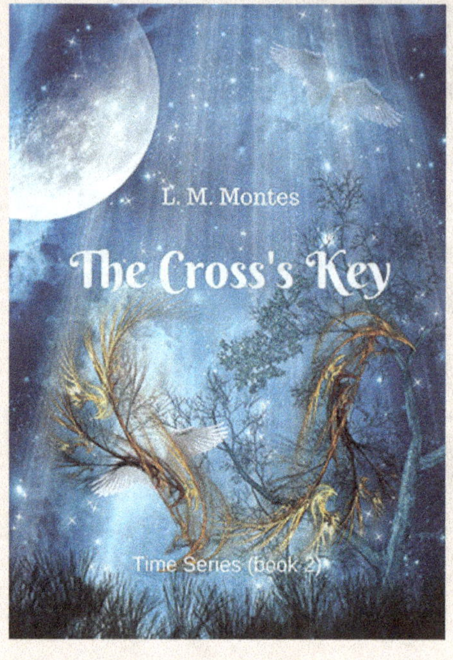

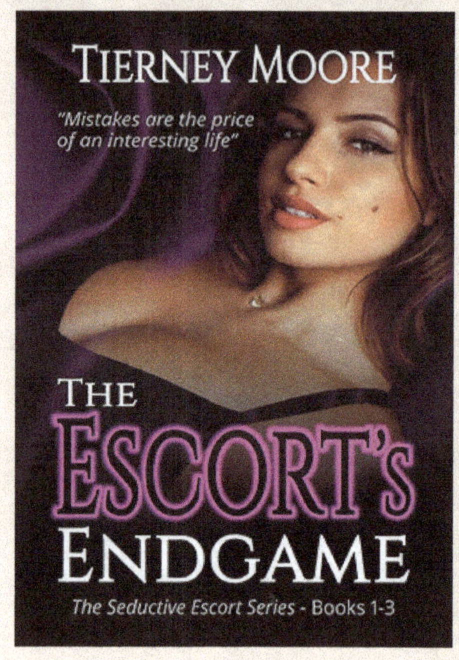

WITHIN THESE WALLS
by Holly Hill Mangin

Within These Walls is a hauntingly beautiful blend of romance and mystery, captivating readers with its evocative writing and intriguing plot.

Within These Walls by Holly Hill Mangin is a captivating blend of romance, mystery, and the supernatural that will keep readers enthralled from start to finish. Set in the eerie and enigmatic Hillfield Manor, the story follows Emma Beckett, a young woman grappling with the recent death of her sister. When Emma is invited to transcribe the family journals at the manor, she eagerly accepts, driven by a long-standing fascination with the haunted estate.

Mangin masterfully creates an atmosphere of suspense and intrigue, with Hillfield Manor almost becoming a character in its own right. The manor's dark history, filled with ghostly sightings and unexplained disappearances, sets the perfect backdrop for the unfolding drama. Emma's journey is both emotional and thrilling as she navigates the manor's secrets and her own grief.

The introduction of Alexander Eason, a ghost who has been dead for three hundred years, adds a unique twist to the narrative. The chemistry between Emma and Alexander is palpable, and their interactions are both poignant and heartwarming. The concept of a secret room where they can appear to each other as more than mere shadows is intriguing and adds an element of urgency to Emma's quest.

While *Within These Walls* is loosely related to "The House on the Lake," it stands firmly on its own, making it accessible to new readers. Fans of gothic romance and supernatural mysteries will find much to love in this book.

Within These Walls is a beautifully crafted tale that explores themes of love, loss, and the enduring power of the past. Holly Hill Mangin has delivered a hauntingly memorable story that will linger with readers long after they turn the final page.

THE CROSS'S KEY
by L. M. Montes

L. M. Montes's The Cross's Key is a thrilling, immersive adventure with rich characters and a gripping, supernatural plot. Highly recommended!

The Cross's Key by L. M. Montes is a masterful continuation of the Time Series that will leave readers on the edge of their seats. From the very first page, Montes weaves a tale of suspense, adventure, and supernatural intrigue that is impossible to put down.

The protagonist, Kyle Stevens, finds himself in a precarious situation after blacking out in the Cave of Treasures and awakening in a different realm. The vivid and historical events unfolding before him are both mesmerizing and horrifying, pulling readers into a world where the past and present collide in the most unexpected ways. Montes's ability to create such a rich and immersive setting is truly commendable.

One of the standout elements of this book is the reappearance of a long-forgotten relic from Kyle's past, which adds layers of mystery and urgency to the narrative. The quest that Kyle must undertake is fraught with danger and moral dilemmas, especially with the malevolent presence of Lord Ladonnis, an evil angel whose sinister plans could cost Kyle his very soul.

Montes excels in character development, particularly with Kyle, whose internal struggles and dedication to his teaching career make him a relatable and compelling hero. The tension between his desire for a normal life and the unavoidable quest he must face is palpable and adds depth to his character.

The pacing of the story is perfect, with each chapter building on the last, leading to a climax that is both satisfying and leaves readers eagerly anticipating the next installment. The blend of historical elements with supernatural themes is executed flawlessly, making *The Cross's Key* a standout in the genre.

In conclusion, *The Cross's Key* is a must-read for fans of supernatural thrillers and historical fiction. L. M. Montes has crafted a gripping and unforgettable tale that will captivate readers from start to finish. Highly recommended!

THE ESCORT'S ENDGAME
by Tierney Moore

A thrilling blend of suspense and steamy romance, The Escort's Endgame captivates with rich characters and evocative settings.

The Escort's Endgame by Tierney Moore is a captivating blend of suspense, romance, and erotica that keeps readers on the edge of their seats. As the fourth installment in "The Seductive Escort Series," this book delves deep into the life of Miranda Stewart, a high-end escort with a dark past and a glamorous present.

Miranda, or Miri, is a complex character who has risen from the depths of homelessness to the heights of luxury, navigating the elite circles of Europe with grace and allure. Her encounters, especially with her female clients, are depicted with a sensuality that is both steamy and emotionally charged. Moore's writing vividly brings to life the opulence of Miri's world, from luxury hotels to superyachts, making for an immersive reading experience.

The suspense element is skillfully woven into the narrative as Miri's past threatens to unravel her carefully constructed life. The introduction of a new, alluring woman adds an unexpected twist, challenging Miri's notions of love and security. The chemistry between them is palpable, adding depth to the erotic scenes that are both explicit and tastefully done.

The Escort's Endgame is more than just a tale of erotic escapades; it's a story of liberation and self-discovery. With its rich character development, thrilling plot, and evocative settings, this book is a must-read for fans of romantic erotica and suspense. Moore's ability to balance steamy romance with a gripping storyline makes this a standout addition to the series.

EDITOR'S CHOICE

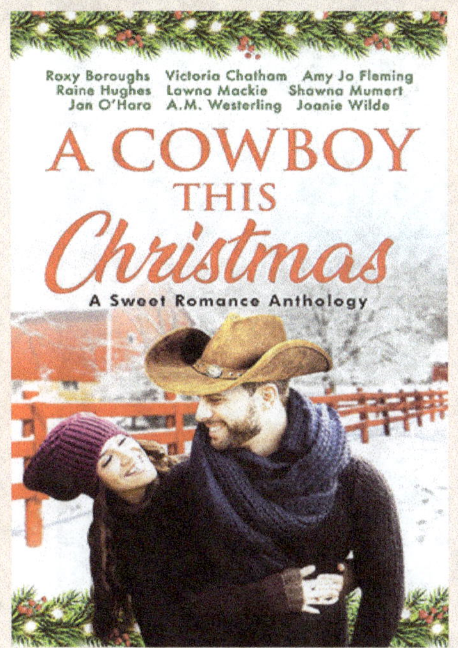

A COWBOY THIS CHRISTMAS
by Roxy Boroughs, Victoria Chatham

THEIR CONNECTICUT CONCUBINE
by Karen Nappa

A NEW DAWNING
by Janice Angelique

A Cowboy This Christmas is a heartwarming anthology, perfect for holiday romance lovers seeking sweet, uplifting, and festive stories.

A captivating blend of romance and erotica, "Their Connecticut Concubine" is an emotional, steamy, and unforgettable journey. Highly recommended!

A New Dawning is a masterful blend of love, family secrets, and redemption, captivating readers with its emotional depth and twists.

A Cowboy This Christmas is a delightful collection of nine heartwarming stories that capture the magic of the holiday season. Each tale, penned by talented authors like Jan O'Hara, Roxy Boroughs, and Victoria Chatham, offers a unique blend of romance, hope, and the spirit of Christmas.

The anthology opens with "The Cowboy's Comeback Christmas," where Jan O'Hara introduces us to a couple with a past, navigating the complexities of second chances. Roxy Boroughs' "Capturing the Christmas Cowboy" follows, bringing a city photographer and a rugged rancher together in a charming, festive setting.

Raine Hughes' *A Rocking Horse Christmas* and A.M. Westerling's *Candy Cane Cowboy* continue the theme of healing and love, each story rich with emotional depth and holiday cheer. Victoria Chatham's *All I Want for Christmas* is a touching narrative about finding family and love in unexpected places.

Lawna Mackie's *Silver Belle*'s Christmas Cowboy adds a dash of adventure, while Shawna Mumert's *My Cowboy, Until Christmas* and Amy Jo Fleming's *Come Home for Christmas, Cowboy*" explore themes of resilience and rekindled love. Joanie Wilde's *A Heart Creek Christmas* rounds out the collection with a tender story of overcoming personal barriers.

A Cowboy This Christmas is a perfect read for anyone looking to immerse themselves in sweet, uplifting romances set against the backdrop of the holiday season. Each story is a testament to the enduring power of love and the magic of Christmas.

Karen Nappa's *Their Connecticut Concubine* is a sizzling, emotional rollercoaster that takes readers on a journey through unexpected romance, intense passion, and heart-wrenching choices.

Elizabeth Brook, the protagonist, steps into a new job expecting to care for an elderly man, only to find herself in the company of a brooding, former hockey player and his equally dominant manager. The chemistry between Elizabeth and her new bosses is palpable from the start, and Nappa masterfully weaves a tale of erotic discovery and emotional depth.

The characters are well-developed, with Elizabeth's transformation from a caregiver to a woman exploring the depths of her desires being particularly compelling. The former hockey player and his manager are not just eye candy; they bring their own complexities and vulnerabilities to the story, making the romantic entanglements feel genuine and deeply engaging.

Nappa's writing is both steamy and sophisticated, balancing the erotic elements with a storyline that keeps you hooked. The world of pain and pleasure that Elizabeth is introduced to is described with a mix of allure and authenticity, making it easy for readers to get lost in the fantasy.

However, the book isn't just about passion. Elizabeth's responsibilities and the tough choices she faces add a layer of realism and emotional weight to the narrative. When the unthinkable happens, the stakes are raised, and readers are left on the edge of their seats, wondering how Elizabeth will navigate her conflicting loyalties.

Their Connecticut Concubine is a captivating read that blends romance, erotica, and drama seamlessly. Karen Nappa has crafted a story that is as heartwarming as it is heart-pounding, making it a must-read for fans of contemporary romance with a daring twist.

A New Dawning by Janice Angelique is a captivating and emotionally charged novel that masterfully intertwines themes of love, family secrets, and personal redemption. From the very first page, Angelique draws readers into the complex lives of her characters, making it nearly impossible to put the book down.

The story centers around Angela, the heiress to a prosperous supermarket chain in the San Fernando Valley. Her life takes an unexpected turn when she meets Martin Richardson, a charming doctor who mistakes her for a cashier. This seemingly innocent misunderstanding sets the stage for a deeply engaging narrative.

Angela's character is both relatable and inspiring. She navigates the challenges of her privileged yet complicated life with grace and determination. Her relationship with Martin is beautifully portrayed, highlighting the nuances of love and trust. Martin, on the other hand, is a man haunted by his past, and his journey towards healing and acceptance is both poignant and compelling.

One of the standout aspects of *A New Dawning* is the intricate family dynamics. Angela's relationship with her domineering mother adds a layer of tension and drama that keeps readers on the edge of their seats. The revelation of a long-kept family secret further intensifies the plot, leading to a dramatic clash between mother and daughter, and sister against sister.

Janice Angelique's writing is both elegant and evocative. She has a talent for creating vivid scenes and complex characters that stay with you long after you've finished the book. The emotional depth and the unexpected twists and turns make *A New Dawning* a truly memorable read.

A New Dawning is a beautifully written novel that explores the complexities of love, family, and personal growth. Janice Angelique has crafted a story that is both heartwarming and heartbreaking, leaving readers with a sense of hope and renewal. This book is a must-read for anyone who enjoys a well-told story with rich character development and a gripping plot. Highly recommended!

PHOTO: *Karl Muller, author of Shadow Works: The House of Mire, delves into the shadows to illuminate the mysteries within.*

Illuminating Shadows

KARL MULLER

Exploring Eschatology, Psychological Depth, and Military Dynamics

Karl Muller discusses inspiration, weaving psychology, biblical influences, faction complexities, and life's impact on storytelling in Shadow Works.

Embarking on an exploration of the mind and beyond, we find ourselves in conversation with Karl Muller, the architect behind the enigmatic novel, Shadow Works: The House of Mire. Muller's life has been a tapestry woven with threads of diversity and intrigue, shaped by a nomadic existence tethered to military service and seasoned with experiences as a counselor and victim advocate. His narrative prowess draws deeply from this reservoir of encounters, infusing his tale with layers of psychological complexity and spiritual resonance.

Rooted in Muller's personal encounters with the inexplicable, Shadow Works emerges as a tapestry interwoven with the threads of eschatology, supernatural conflict, and the machinations of power. Muller's candid revelation regarding the genesis of his novel unveils a journey that spans over two decades, from the initial conception during college days to its resurrection amidst the upheaval of a global pandemic. This serendipitous revival breathed life into a tale that had long lingered in the shadows of memory.

The interplay of psychological elements within Muller's narrative is a testament to his astute observation of human dynamics, honed through years of service in the military trenches and the trenches of the human psyche. Drawing parallels between military deployments and the unfolding drama within his book, Muller illuminates the intricacies of group dynamics amidst the chaos of conflict, lending authenticity and depth to his characters' struggles.

Central to the fabric of Shadow Works is the concept of Eschaton, a term laden with biblical connotations of apocalypse and divine will. Muller deftly navigates this celestial terrain, intertwining the cosmic narrative with the mundane lives of his characters, blurring the lines between the extraordinary and the ordinary.

At the heart of Muller's narrative beats the age-old dichotomy of light versus darkness, embodied in the conflict between The Flock and The Coven. Yet, true to the complexities of human nature, Muller delves beyond mere archetypes, imbuing each faction with layers of motive and moral ambiguity. In this dance of shadows and light, heroes and villains emerge not as monoliths

but as flawed, multifaceted beings driven by personal agendas and collective ideologies.

Muller's own odyssey, marked by countless relocations and cultural collisions, serves as the crucible from which his storytelling prowess emerges. Through his characters' diverse backstories, linguistic nuances, and geographic tapestry, Muller paints a vivid tableau reflective of his own kaleidoscopic journey through life.

As we unravel the layers of Shadow Works, guided by Muller's insightful reflections, we are beckoned into a world where the boundaries between the seen and the unseen blur, and where the shadows hold secrets that may yet shape the destiny of all who dare to tread its murky depths.

What inspired you to delve into the themes of eschatology, supernatural conflict, and the manipulation of power structures in your novel SHADOW WORKS: The House of Mire?

The novel was inspired by some weird things that happened to me when I was younger, things that some would consider paranormal. I assigned intent to these experiences for creative purposes, which gave rise to the notion of good vs evil and this became the foundation of the book. There are religious elements throughout the novel, but it is not a religious book.

I created the story and character concepts for the book in 2001 while attending college. I didn't have the time to dedicate to writing at the time, so I pushed the project aside. The pages resurfaced twenty years later during a COVID garage cleaning. I read the pages, still found them interesting, and began writing the story.

With your background in counseling and victim advocacy, how did you weave psychological elements into the narrative of your book?

I crafted the narrative with a

military deployment in mind. Military personnel frequently find themselves in groups of strangers and given tasks they must work on cooperatively while overcoming barriers that stand in their way. Playing offense one day and defense the next. It is controlled chaos, but somehow works. The group dynamics that emerge from these scenarios is very interesting to witness and I applied these characteristics to the story.

Could you discuss the significance of the term Eschaton in your story, and how it influences the characters and the unfolding events?

The biblical term, Eschaton refers to the end of the world. This speaks to a celestial awareness of God's will, that the world is in the beginning stage of Armageddon. The big game is about to begin, however the characters are unaware of this event.

The conflict between The Flock and The Coven seems to represent a battle between light and darkness. What motivated you to explore such dichotomies, and how do you portray the complexities within each faction?

I started with the ageless tale of good vs evil, and reduced this theme into factions while placing the narrative in the modern day. Much of the plot was informed by my consideration of these groups' goals as well as the personal incentives of each character. Bad actors aren't hiding in shadows any longer and good actors no longer turn the other cheek.

Your diverse life experiences, including military service and frequent relocation, likely provided unique perspectives. How did these experiences shape your storytelling approach and the development of your characters?

I spent the first 48 years of my life on the road moving from one place to the next due to military relocations: as a child dependent, an active-duty military member, and as a husband to a military spouse, resulting in over 35 moves and ten years living abroad. While tumultuous, the experience provided an abundance of cultural and spiritual fulfillment to draw from when writing. This influence is reflected in character backstories, language, geography, historical events, and aspects of my professional career.

Unveiling History's Tapestry

LEE SWANSON

A Life Shaped by Treks, Travels and Literary Legends

Lee Swanson discusses crafting historical fiction, creating strong female characters, and balancing authenticity with suspense in his acclaimed novels.

Lee Swanson's journey from soldier to scholar has been as adventurous and diverse as the historical landscapes he vividly brings to life in his novels. His fascination with medieval history, houned during his years living in Germany and England, permeates every page of his work, blending meticulous research with captivating storytelling.

In our exclusive interview with Swanson, we delve into the intricate tapestry of his writing process, where historical accuracy intertwines seamlessly with imaginative narrative. His superlative *No Man is Her Master* series introduces readers to Christina Kohl, a fiercely independent protagonist navigating the treacherous waters of 14th-century Europe. Swanson reveals the inspirations behind Christina's character, born from a desire to defy the limitations placed upon medieval women, and the challenges he faced in crafting her compelling arc amidst a backdrop of political intrigue and danger.

With each novel, Swanson paints a vivid portrait of medieval society, populated by richly developed characters drawn from the ranks of merchants and nobility. His latest instalment, She Serves the Realm, delves deeper into themes of love, duty, and sacrifice against the backdrop of civil unrest, inviting readers to join Christina on her journey of self-discovery and resilience.

Through Swanson's storytelling prowess, readers are transported across centuries, experiencing the trials and triumphs of characters whose struggles resonate across time. Join us as we explore the captivating world of Lee Swanson, where history comes alive through the power of fiction.

Your background in European History, particularly focusing on the Hansa, seems to heavily influence your writing. How do you blend historical accuracy with fictional storytelling in your novels?

It's essential to be aware of the facts first and then move the characters to fit the historical reality. Historical accuracy is just as important as crafting an excellent story in writing historical fiction. I am painstaking in my research, doing my best to provide my readers with the authentic flavour of the times in which the novel is set. The final days of Piers Gaveston are well documented; consequently, Christina Kohl's movements and interactions in She Serves the Realm are shaped by the necessity of her being in particular places at specific times.

In "She Serves the Realm," Lee Swanson masterfully continues Christina Kohl's gripping journey, weaving a tapestry of loyalty, love, and peril against the backdrop of Edward II's turbulent reign. Swanson's vivid prose transports readers into a world where courage and cunning collide, leaving them yearning for more.

Christina Kohl, the protagonist of your *No Man is Her Master* series, defies societal norms of her time by seeking adventure and independence. What inspired you to create such a strong and unconventional female character set in the 14th century?

I set out to craft a female character who would not simply be defined by the men in her life. This proved difficult, as there were few opportunities for medieval women to live independently. So, I cheated by having Christina assume her brother's identity. This allowed her to experience life with the freedom enjoyed by her male counterparts, but expressed from a woman's perspective.

In Her Perilous Game, Christina faces political intrigue and danger. How do you approach crafting suspenseful plots while maintaining authenticity to the historical setting?

Her Perilous Game is set in 1310, as King Edward II mounts an expedition to the Scottish borders in a futile attempt to force Robert the Bruce to battle. Christina sails to Berwick-upon-Tweed to warn her friend, the Earl of Cornwall, of a supposed scheme against his life. The real-life plotting and peril facing Gaveston during this time made a believable backdrop for incorporating Christina's story in tandem with the earl's own?

She Serves the Realm introduces readers to Christina's complex journey as she navigates her identity, love, and loyalty amidst the political turmoil of Edward II's reign. What challenges did you face in portraying this turbulent historical period?

A challenge was in portraying Piers Gaveston as a sympathetic character. Throughout the first three novels in the series, the unlikely friendship between the teenaged Christina and the powerful Earl of Cornwall grows, although it is rarely central to the plot. In She Serves the Realm, Gaveston is a major character whose predicaments drive the development of the story. I want readers to discover that the man Christina has grown to love and admire is very different than the despicable caricature commonly depicted in history.

Your novels feature richly developed characters drawn from the lives of merchants and nobility in medieval Europe. How do you research and develop these characters to bring them to life on the page?

In creating characters for my novels, I try to base them initially on people I have discovered in nonfiction sources. For instance, there is a great collection of the correspondence of Hildebrand Veckinchusen that provides great insight into the life of a Hansa merchant of the early 15th century. Then I flesh out the character with attributes of someone I had read about in fiction, seen in films, or even people I know in real life. After these traits are established they just seem to take on a life of their own.

Your latest novel, She Serves the Realm, delves into themes of love, duty, and sacrifice against the backdrop of civil unrest. What do you hope readers take away from Christina's story and her experiences serving both her own desires and the demands of the realm?

I hope readers view Christina as a person who tries to stay true to herself. She is not infallible; she makes mistakes and sometimes suffers for them. She can be overly impetuous, which has at times placed her and her companions in mortal danger. But she also has a good heart and a strong sense of right and wrong. Not only is she willing to come to the aid of those she holds dear, but will also defend those who have wronged her when they are treated unjustly. I think it is also important to show that romantic love between two women is a universal truth that transcends history.

A Journey into Pet Nutrition with
STEPHANIE KROL
Exploring the Intersection of Education, Publishing, and Animal Wellness

Dr. Stephanie Krol, a global authority, shares her journey from academia to pet nutrition advocacy, challenging misconceptions and empowering pet owners.

Stephanie Krol is not your average authority in Higher Education Administration. With over 25 years of global experience, she has left an indelible mark not only in academia but also in the realms of publishing, pet nutrition, and animal wellness. As a distinguished professor, speaker, curriculum developer, and dean, Dr. Krol has navigated the complex landscape of education with unparalleled expertise, even co-owning a national real estate school. But her influence doesn't stop there.

Delving into the world of publishing, Stephanie has emerged as a #1 best-selling author and the visionary founder of Riley-Infinity & Lemniscate-Infinity Press, offering boutique publishing services. Her commitment to animal health led her to become a certified raw dog food nutrition specialist, pet health coach, and functional medicine practitioner. Her impact extends beyond words on paper; she actively advocates for the well-being of pets, leveraging her extensive background in equestrianism and veterinary technology.

In a recent interview with Reader's House Magazine, Dr. Krol sheds light on her journey into pet nutrition and wellness, a path born from personal experience and a desire to leave a lasting legacy. Her insights challenge common misconceptions, urging pet owners to question conventional wisdom and prioritize their furry companions' health. Through meticulous research and a dedication to education, Stephanie empowers pet parents to make informed decisions, advocating for a future where holistic pet care is readily accessible.

As the landscape of pet nutrition continues to evolve, Dr. Krol envisions a world where pet health coaches and nutritionists play a pivotal role in guiding owners towards optimal care. Her mission is clear: to champion a paradigm shift in how we nourish and care for our beloved pets, ensuring they thrive for years to come. Through her expertise and unwavering dedication, Stephanie Krol stands as a beacon of knowledge and compassion in the realm of animal wellness.

What inspired you to delve into the topic of pet nutrition and wellness?

What you read in my book started right there in the vet office when I refused to accept their prognosis and took my dog's health into my own hands. It's super scary, but when you refuse to let your dog go, you take big risks to get big rewards! It turns out my method; I chose was the most healing and least risky, but it sure didn't feel that way with all the traditional advice I was getting so I sought the top people in Holistic Veterinary Medicine, Homeopathy, and Chinese Medicine to see what my options were, and it turned out, that my choices were the safest, least risky, and most focused on health, wellness, pain removal, and healing.

I am a Dr., educator, functional medicine practitioner, and a researcher, and I have put all my decades of experience in research and examination to find real solutions for pet owners, not to mention, my years of coaching humans into healthier lifestyles, and being a Vet Tech. in my first job for three years, and avid Raw Dog Food Nutrition Specialist, also played a role in what I found. Having a doctorate of any kind really, certainly helps read, run, and convey research and statistics and my terminal degreed had many such courses, so I was able to weed through everything as quick as possible to save my boy.

I applied this experience to my dog. When I saw what it did for him, I became convinced that I needed to share it with the world. There are too many dogs out there right now who are suffering. They're itchy, inflamed, losing the bounce in their step, and prematurely aging. Every meal of overly processed, cleverly marketed commercial pet feed, every toxin we put into their systems and on them because it's convenient, and every so-called treatment, pill, or potion we give them can be stealing their health and shortening their years. That's not okay. You and I can do something about it—for our dogs.

The other reason for the book was purely mine. I had realized one day and was asking myself what matters, did all the education, working three jobs through college, going full time, being a Dean of Schools, Professor and educator for a couple decades all now matter, and when we get to that forty mark we all start asking what matters and what did matter and after thinking about all I have done, I started asking myself, how does one leave a legacy, and how does anyone know once we are gone after a certain period that we were here, and I came up with paying gobs of money to put my name on a library or hospital or funny enough, to write a book that goes on to infinity, and it just so happens I ended up naming my publishing services company with the word infinity, and I just realized that, for different reasons riley-infinity.com, so it's amazing how we end up where we are at times doing what we are doing, and as we all know, books go on to infinity, because when we go we have to will them to someone for the royalties, so that's also why I wrote my book, to leave a legacy and I felt it was the reason I was here in this world, to help reverse pain and disease in pets and prevent it before it happens.

How did you go about conducting your research for this book?

Initially, I sought the top people in Holistic Veterinary Medicine even internationally, Homeopathy, and Chinese Medicine to see what my options were, and it turned out, that my choices were the safest, least risky, and most focused on health, wellness, pain removal, and real healing. I then applied what I learned from my doctorate, weeding through the research, from everywhere I could find on how to reverse disease states, what causes it, and how the body heals. I used my certifications in Raw Dog Food Nutrition, Functional Medicine, and previous knowledge as a Vet Tech. I have

had a dog since I was born as I arrived home to my first puppy right from the hospital, and have had one my entire life, minus on year when I moved to another state. I have also had two horses from like 10 years on and rode horses and competed professionally from seven years on for 25 years, so I also had more pet knowledge, unfortunately it was in the traditional sense, so I really had to quickly learn what was the most appropriate thing to do, to heal my boy.

Can you share any personal anecdotes or experiences that influenced your approach to pet care?

Originally, I was very traditional minded; I had three degrees from traditional schools, was schooled in quantitative methods in my doctorate, and really believed testing and application, and vaccination and antibiotics were necessary. I wasn't until I know how well I had taken care of my boy and started titering at three years old and in fact I had run a genetic test as he had been getting allergies, and it showed that out of 300 different genetic issues that cause disease, he had none. So what I was being told by top veterinarians, of which I knew were showing me test after test, needle biopsy results, and ultrasounds, just made little sense. I was also not given straightforward answers and was told, well, it's called the practice of medicine for a reason, and a light went off.

You see, he was fed the best organic raw dog foods, stopped unnecessarily vaccinating him early on, gave proof of titers instead and he had perfect filtered water, no chemicals in the house or in the backyard, and I even washed his feed from subdivision walks from other people who spray their yards and they told me out of nowhere at age 11, and also being the first time he was ever sick that he had 3-4 months to live with or without surgery and if I don't do surgery to remove his spleen it will kill him, and while they are in there they will check the liver etc. That was really it verbatim, so none of it made sense, and he was the type of dog that would walk into a clinic immediately traumatized from a vaccination experience when he was just a baby a veterinarian gave him a shot in the leg and he was in pain for two days barely walking and from then on it was panting, sweating, drooling and well, I know surgery, a clinic, fighting with them to let me stay would be nearly impossible and I

really felt that in itself might kill him more. So, that's when I delved, into learning everything I could, setting up consultations, researching journals and medical testing, literally everything I could find and settled on a species appropriate diet to heal him while removing all toxins, and taking the drag off his body so he could heal, and he did.

for people too, because just because someone with a degree says, it's safe and has a white coat, doesn't simply mean they are right, the test could be wrong, the data could be skewed, you could have someone with little experience in that area or new and they could do their best, but I always suggest 2nd and 3rd opinions for all things because that is exactly what it is, is an "opinion" and people forget that when someone is nice to them. It's so critical and important for pet owners to ask questions, get informed and do not follow someone just because they are nice, have a white coat and a degree, they really have to get the data, the understanding behind how they got there and what basis they are forming their "opinion".

My book addresses a lot of these misconceptions and more, as well as vaccinations, raw feeding, species appropriate feeding, how to biologically feed and why, even the stages of cancer creation to raw bones and many other items even for puppies and cats, and I do my best, to provide the latest data and research from top journals and professionals and veterinary schools, so people can learn the knowledge, but most importantly, learn why they need to ask the questions, get informed so they can make the best decisions for their pet. I certainly tell my story, but I don't tell anyone to do anything. I educate, provide research and fill in all the blanks traditional care misses and a lot of it is because it's not their job truly. Many, many people are misinformed on what type of veterinarian to go to for what, meaning, broken legs, uncontrolled bleeding, surgeries, drugs and vaccinations among other things obviously and specialties, well that's traditional medicine, and health, wellness, nutrition, then you're looking for anything from a dog or cat coach, to a holistic veterinarian, or a raw dog food nutritionist specialist like myself, but that's also why you have to ask questions and be informed so you know where to go to help your pet also, because unfortunately in the field clinicians aren't educating clients when they come in or sending them home with things to read or explaining these differences, they roll right into the issues and the appointment rather than asking first, is this client in the right spot, is this issue really for me to solve and that's the biggest thing missing in the industry and the educating of pet parents, so I have attempted to do so with my book, so pet parents know where to go, for what and to the correct person if they are looking for true healing, nutrition or drugs. For example, Europe and other countries combined have pet nutrition as part of their curriculum as opposed to the US with just four, so it's easy to memorize those things or look them up before your consultations, that way you also know who to go to for what.

In your opinion, what are the key factors pet owners should consider when selecting food for their furry friends?

Is it commercialized pet feed?

Is it raw food?

Is it cooked food?

Then, where does it come from, is it organic, is it human grade, or pet grade or does it have synthetic undigestible supplements and what all of all of that means, then they can determine what it all means, and if what they are putting in and on their dog is disease creating or health creating and if they evaluate foods that way, and what is really best for their loving pet, they will easily know how to keep them happy, healthy and bouncing for joy, because at minimum that's certainly what our pets deserve for all the love, loyalty and devotion they give us, not to mention the items we mess up accidentally and they forgive us.

How do you envision the future of pet nutrition evolving, and how can pet owners stay informed about the latest developments in this field?

Gosh, pet nutrition is evolving constantly, even if you googled raw dog food, or fresh pet food or maybe even organic raw dog food, you will see so many options, all of course better than those dried, synthetic, dehydrating foods often available on the cheap. I do think people are opening their eyes more to what they see and questioning many things now, whether it's for them or their pets, so this is a super time to truly educate pet parents as they are much more open to it and seeking valuable information.

I'd love to see a pet health coach at every traditional clinic, as you may have noticed a lot more, in traditional medicine for people. Pet coaches, Pet or Veterinary nutritionists, Raw Dog Food Nutrition Specialists, Pet Food Consultants, Animal Wellness Coaches, and the like, so people could go there as needed and get informed to make the very best decisions for what they put on and in their pet because it certainly matters as it does for us, we are eating and doing things that create disease or health and wellness and it's no different for our pets!

Unveiling Desire
DAMIEN DSOUL
Exploring Erotic Literature, Liberation, and Taboos

Damien Dsoul's interview delves into marriage complexities, African dangers, sexual adventures, and hidden desires, highlighting themes of exploration and liberation.

In our exclusive interview with Damien Dsoul, the mastermind behind a diverse array of erotic literature, we delve deep into the intricacies of desire, liberation, and exploration. From the complex dynamics of marriage in *Mary's Addiction* to the perilous journey through militant kidnappers in *The Story of Thaddeus Black*, Dsoul's narratives confront societal taboos head-on. In *Southern Hospitality: Horny Wives of Pinopolis*, and The Seduction Game, he navigates the clandestine worlds of sexual exploration and secret desires. *Wife Breeding Team and Other Stories* and *The Suburban Wives Club* unveil the multifaceted layers of interracial fetishes and communal liberation. Join us as we unravel the enigma of human desire through Dsoul's captivating storytelling.

How do the characters in Mary's Addiction navigate the complexities of their evolving desires and the strains it places on their marriage?

For the two main characters, Donald and Mary Clauston, their relationship harbours an underlying strain in their marriage that had been building over time.

Mary has been harbouring feelings of underappreciation and neglect from her husband, Donald, who seemed indifferent to his wife's inner plight. When Mary allows herself to get sexually used by the three black male burglars, the sexual encounter, whilst initially unwelcoming, was what burst the dam of concern for her. Mary starts seeing herself as a newly liberated woman, someone who has, so far, neglected addressing her sexual desires due to Donald never showing any feeling of wanting towards her.

For Donald, the opposite is the case. He is appalled by Mary's demeanour whereas she harbours no thought of restrain as she then seeks to explore her sex, and dare her husband to realise what's been missing in their marriage. Donald is hard-headed, as any husband would be, but when he realises other friends/neighbours have been indulging in such kinky lifestyle, does it compels him to start viewing things from her perspective.

In The Story of Thaddeus Black, what challenges does the protagonist face as he delves into the dangerous world of militant kidnappers in Africa?

Thaddeus Black is clueless about what to expect when traveling to Nigeria, to find the missing American teenagers he's tasked to locate. He knows he's diving into an underbelly of criminal activity, but it's beyond whatever he has encountered back home in America. He has unprepared to realise how connected the Black Path militants are with the socio-political situation in the country.

Things turn dire when he gets kidnapped and sent to a slave camp, Camp Kuta, where he encounters a large number of Caucasian persons who had long been kidnapped and converted into sex slaves. He undergoes an ancient Yoruba initiation rite that declares him to be a reincarnated Nigerian deity. Thaddeus does his best to play along while scheming for clandestine ways of escaping the camp, and protecting his girlfriend who undertook the mission with him.

What themes of exploration and liberation are present in Southern Hospitality: Horny Wives of Pinopolis as the protagonist encounters a series of sexually adventurous encounters?

The couples residing in the upper-class neighbourhood of Pinopolis share a strong sense of community friendship that enables them to maintain and explore their kinky lifestyle without fear of outside exposure.

The book's theme of inner-world exposes how couples maintain a close-knit group that's far removed from the outside society. The couples/wives that share this group utilise it to shed themselves of their sexual inhibitions, and to maintain a close sisterhood-like fraternity that goes unnoticed by the world at large.

How does The Seduction Game explore the dynamics of desire within a marriage as the main character ventures into a secret life of escorting?

The book expresses the sentiment of hidden sexual motives that are often prevalent in a majority of marriages that often lie hidden under the surface. For the main character in the book, her marriage is a typical picture-perfect sort of marriage. It's not until she strays into a newfound lifestyle by venturing into escort services alongside her best friend that inevitably unlocks hidden templates of sexual pleasure the likes of which she and her spouse haven't explored before.

In Wife Breeding Team and Other Stories, how do the different tales contribute to the broader theme of interracial/cuckold fetish and the exploration of untapped desires?

Each story comprises of cuckold tales showcased from multiple perspectives: from the wife, the husband, including the wife's would-be lover(s). They showcase a dynamic range of emotions and motivations aroused from dynamic range of couples, including interracial and romantic entanglements between unrelated characters.

What transformations do the characters undergo in "The Suburban Wives Club" as they embark on a journey of sexual liberation within their community?

I consider each female character in the book like specific Marvel comic book heroes who inevitably come together to form a team due to their yearning sexual wants. Their individual need is what enables them to bond into a formidable commune to share their sexual pleasures with and/or without their husbands' approval. It was fun to enable each character express their sexual range individually as well together as a group.

Marlena Frank, acclaimed author of "The Seeking," discusses her inspiration and creative process in an exclusive interview with Reader's House Magazine.

Unraveling Shadows with

MARLENA FRANK

Exploring Inspiration, World-Building, and Character Dynamics in "The Seeking"

Marlena Frank discusses "The Seeking," drawing from dreams, wildlife inspiration, and familial dynamics, crafting a gripping tale of resilience and revelation

Embarking on a journey into the world of literature often means venturing into realms where the ordinary merges with the extraordinary, where characters traverse landscapes both familiar and fantastical. Marlena Frank, a luminary in the realm of young adult fantasy and horror, invites readers into such realms with her gripping narratives, each page a portal to worlds both wondrous and eerie.

With several bestsellers under her belt and a slew of accolades from platforms like Readers' Favorite, Frank has carved a niche for herself in the literary landscape. Her latest venture, "The Seeking," beckons readers into a realm where the line between dreams and reality blurs, where the forest teems with creatures both enchanting and ominous, and where a young protagonist named Dahlia navigates a labyrinth of ritualistic challenges and unsettling truths.

In a recent interview with Reader's House Magazine, Frank delves into the genesis of "The Seeking," unraveling the threads of inspiration that wove together to form its tapestry. Rooted in a vivid dream that gripped her imagination, Frank's narrative unfolds with the surrealism of a haunting reverie, drawing readers into a world where every shadow conceals a secret, and every step leads deeper into the unknown.

Central to Frank's narrative is Dahlia, a protagonist whose journey mirrors the author's own penchant for resilience and determination. Through Dahlia's eyes, readers witness a world fraught with peril and possibility, where the bonds of family and the solace of love serve as beacons in the darkness.

But it's not just the characters that captivate in Frank's tale; it's the world itself, meticulously crafted with an eye for detail and an ear for atmosphere. From the eerie depths of the forest to the enigmatic presence of the Gray People, every facet of Carra

breathes with a life of its own, inviting readers to lose themselves in its mysteries.

As the interview unfolds, Frank peels back the layers of her narrative, offering insights into the dynamics that drive her characters and the challenges she faced in bringing their story to life. From the intricacies of world-building to the pulse-pounding crescendo of the novel's climax, Frank's journey is as riveting as the tale she weaves.

In "The Seeking," Marlena Frank beckons readers to embark on a journey into the unknown, where every page is a step closer to unraveling the secrets that lie shrouded in darkness. With her trademark blend of fantasy and horror, Frank reminds us that sometimes, the most terrifying truths are the ones we seek to uncover..

What inspired the concept of "The Seeking" and the ritualistic challenges faced by Dahlia and her community?

The initial inspiration came from a vivid dream I had. The scene with the Ritual came almost directly from it, straight down to the creatures watching from the shadows and the horrible feeling that something was very wrong. When I sat down to write the book, I crafted a world and characters that I wanted to lead to the bizarre and unsettling moment. I wanted that scene to feel surreal, dreamlike, and unsettling, and I think it delivers.

How did you approach the world-building in your novel, particularly in creating the eerie atmosphere of the forest and the creatures within it?

When I sat down to craft the creatures of the forest, I drew inspiration from the book Writing Monsters by Philip Athans. I created monsters out of things I found terrifying or unsettling, things that would prevent the people of Carra from stepping out of line. As a wildlife enthusiast, I honestly had a great time creating these nightmarish creatures.

The Gray People were more subtle. I wanted them to feel like something that stepped out of folklore, something that shouldn't exist but does. That you would have to get used to living your life with creatures staring at you from the forest all the time, never really knowing if they were gentle or monstrous, is both terrifying and fascinating to me. Setting the world around Halloween just added to the spooky atmosphere.

Dahlia is a compelling protagonist; what qualities did you want her character to embody, and how did she evolve throughout the story?

Dahlia is the middle child of the Priest family, much like I was as a child. But the dynamics of her relationship with her siblings aren't very good. She wants to protect her young brother, Dameon, so she's always trying to keep him safe against a town that wants to capture him. Her older brother, Darik, thinks he has everything figured out, but his hubris ends up being his downfall. Dahlia doesn't trust people enough to stay with anyone during the Seeking. She doesn't want to risk her girlfriend, Bisa's, life, or burden her mother with finding a place to hide her. She's independent, determined, and sometimes a little too focused on her own goals to see the real danger in her plans.

At the beginning of the story, she takes a lot for granted. She thinks she can hide from everyone and that her hiding place is foolproof. She can't imagine the real danger that she and her family are in. As everything

falls apart around her, Dahlia sees the horror she has lived under for so long. She rejects it and is determined to find an alternative path forward. She loses that naivety that she once had and takes hold of her future with both hands.

The relationships between characters, such as Dahlia and Bisa, are central to the narrative. Can you discuss the importance of these dynamics in the story?

Bisa is Dahlia's strength. She has the independence that Dahlia wishes she could have. Bisa is raising her little brother on her own meager income. She's happy with the life she now has, the life that Dahlia helped her fight to get. While Dahlia loves her own family, the family's reputation, their power plays, and all the demands of being part of an Exalted family hold her back from who she wants to be.

As everything falls down around them, they rely on each other even more. Bisa grounds Dahlia with reason. She supports her, and she is always there to hold her when tears inevitably come.

The Gray People add a fascinating layer to the story. What was the inspiration behind their inclusion, and what role do they play in the world of "The Seeking"?

I wanted the Gray People to be mysterious. They remind me of nature spirits at first, treated like folklore or deities. Nobody knows why they are there or what interest they really have in the people of Carra. All they have is the tradition of the Ritual and the promise of their protection. The more Dahlia learns,

the more the veil of mystery gets pulled back on these people. There are clues scattered throughout the book about how they came about and how the world wasn't always this way. But to Dahlia, this is the truth and has always been the truth. Until everything falls apart.

The climax of the novel is intense and action-packed. Without giving away spoilers, what challenges did you face in writing such a pivotal moment?

As with any action scene, especially one with so much build-up as in The Seeking, the trouble is trying to make sure the action makes sense. I want to make sure every character gets a perspective and a chance to be seen. But also, the ferocity of the adversary is important. If they aren't terrifying, threatening, and tearing into the protagonist, then the climax wouldn't have the impact it does. A hero is only as good as their villain, and the big bad in The Seeking is truly awful. When pushed against the wall, Dahlia must make a terrible decision and deal with the consequences.

PHOTO: *Terry Overton: Retired professor, award-winning author, and storyteller extraordinaire, blending education and faith through the power of storytelling*

From Classroom to Cathedral - The Journey of
TERRY OVERTON
A Retrospective on Education, Faith, and the Power of Storytelling

Terry Overton, retired professor, discusses her transition from academia to Christian fiction, blending teaching, faith, and award-winning storytelling

Embarking on a journey through the corridors of Terry Overton's life and work reveals a profound dedication to education, psychology, and faith. With a repertoire spanning from the realms of academia to the realms of storytelling, Overton's multifaceted career showcases a remarkable blend of expertise and creativity. A retired university professor boasting accolades in educational and school psychology, Overton's contributions to the field have left an indelible mark. Yet, it is her foray into the world of Christian literature that truly illuminates her passion for teaching and storytelling.

From the very foundation of her career, teaching has been the cornerstone of Overton's endeavours.

Beginning in the trenches of public schools, she honed her focus on the individual learning needs of children, a principle that would remain steadfast throughout her professional journey. Transitioning to the realm of higher education, she expanded her scope to encompass the provision of educational strategies and psychological insights to aspiring educators and counsellors. As a dean and department chair, her mentorship extended beyond the classroom, nurturing the growth of faculty and administrators alike.

Now, in her role as a Christian author, Overton's commitment to teaching finds new expression. Through a diverse array of literary endeavours, she endeavours to impart Scripture and Christian values to readers of all ages. Whether weaving tales of time travel in the Newton Chronicles or exploring themes of resilience in The Journey: The Underground Book Readers, Overton seamlessly integrates her faith into narratives that captivate and inspire.

In Legends of the Donut Shop, Overton draws from personal experiences and family stories to craft a narrative imbued with themes of second chances, forgiveness, and the transformative power of faith.

Inspired by the camaraderie of her late father and his comrades, she breathes life into characters whose journeys mirror her own encounters with faith and redemption.

Balancing the rigors of academic writing with the artistry of storytelling is no small feat, yet Overton navigates this terrain with finesse. Drawing upon her background in educational psychology, she infuses her Christian fiction with a depth of understanding and a commitment to authenticity. Through meticulous research and consultation with theological experts, she ensures that her narratives resonate with readers on both intellectual and spiritual levels.

Overton's literary endeavours have garnered acclaim, with awards such as the Firebird Book Awards and the International Book Award Finalist lending credence to her work. Yet,

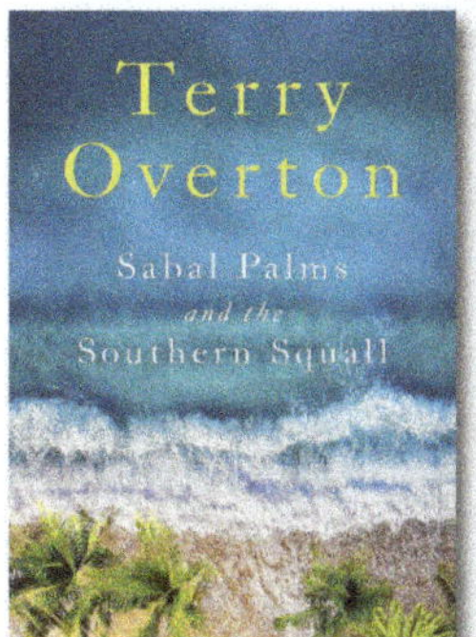

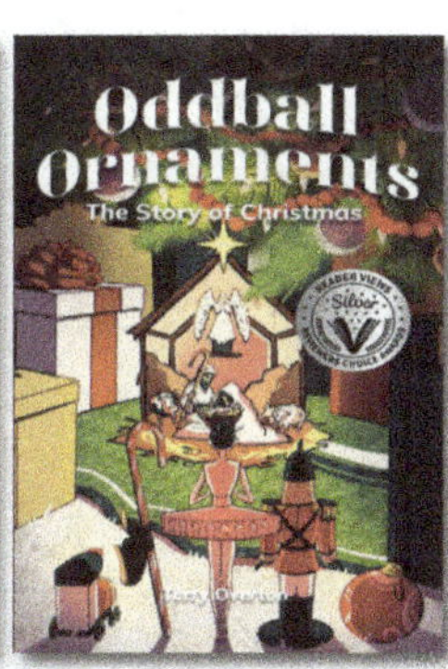

Legends of the Donut Shop: A captivating tale of faith, forgiveness, and second chances, by award-winning author Terry Overton.

beyond the accolades lies a deeper mission—to share the good news and grow the church through the power of storytelling. With each book she pens, Overton seeks to ignite a spark of faith in the hearts of her readers, guiding them on a journey of discovery and transformation.

As she continues to chart new territories in the realm of Christian literature, Overton's unwavering dedication to teaching and storytelling serves as a beacon of inspiration. Through her words, she invites readers to embark on a journey of faith, hope, and endless possibility—a journey that promises to leave an indelible mark on the soul.

Your background in educational and school psychology is extensive, with experience ranging from teaching to serving as a college dean. How has this background influenced your approach to writing Christian books and devotionals?

Teaching has been at the heart of all my professional positions and continues to be the centre of my writing. Teaching in public schools my focus was on individual learning needs of children. Teaching at the university level changed my focus to

Diane M. Dresback, award-winning author, and filmmaker, shares insights into her creative process and storytelling journey in an exclusive interview.

providing sound educational strategies, psychological, and behavioural techniques for teachers, counsellors, and school psychologists. As a university department chair and dean,

my focus was mentoring faculty and young administrators. Now, as a Christian author, I strive to teach Scripture and Christian values. This might mean incorporating Bible history into a time travel series (Newton Chronicles), teaching the true meaning of Christmas using animated ornaments (The Oddball Ornaments), or teaching about Heaven and standing up for what is right (Legends of the Donut Shop).

Your book The Journey: The Underground Book Readers explores themes of resilience and perseverance in a dystopian world. What inspired you to write this series, and how do you integrate Christian values into the narrative?

Last year I interviewed school and community librarians about the current attempts to censor classic literature and Christian books in their own libraries and administrative structure. Their testimony inspired me to write a series that would place young readers in a world where books were banned, schools destroyed, and churches burned. The parents of the teen characters had been taken or "disappeared." This left the teens and preteens in a world that would be of their own making. They were determined to continue to read, study, and even have their own church in an underground cavern. The children and teens in the series faced threats at every turn and had to rely on each other and the guidance from God through Scripture for survival.

Legends of the Donut Shop delves into themes of second chances, life lessons, and forgiveness. Can you discuss

how your own experiences and beliefs inform the messages conveyed in this book?

This book was inspired by my late father and his buddies, all veterans of the Korean War, WWII, or Vietnam, who met each week at the local donut shop for fellowship and fun. Tales of my father-in-law, and my son-in-law, a rancher in Texas, are also incorporated in the story. The opening scene, a near-death experience, is based on my own near-death experience from thirty years ago. In the story, a teenage boy has a near-death experience and goes back in time to his childhood visits to the donut shop with his grandfather. He hears the same stories he heard before but this time, each story conveys a meaning he now understands. He at last embraces the meaning of Scripture and the Bible he had only superficially absorbed as a child. The same experience of renewed faith happened to me, and to many others who have had near-death experiences. Following this experience, I understood life after death, and I am secure in knowing where I will be following the transition from life to death and Heaven. My dad passed from Covid before he ever read the book. He had seen the cover and three weeks later, he contracted Covid. My mother passed the day before my dad. Dad's buddies from the donut shop were the pallbearers at the funeral. I was blessed to give each on a copy of the book inspired by their group and my dad.

As a retired university professor, you've authored textbooks and journal articles in the fields of special education and school psychology. How do you balance the academic rigor of your professional writing with the storytelling elements of your Christian fiction?

Research was always something I loved about academia. In Christian writing, I conduct similar research on Biblical history, Jewish heritage, world geography, world history, the history of the United States, and historic documents. Authentic Christian fiction requires research. This must be carefully weighed with theological leanings and theological works. When possible, I consult with others who can provide more insight (Rabbis of Jewish faith and heritage, Messianic Jewish Rabbis, Christian pastors, etc.).

Your books have received several awards, including the Firebird Book Awards and the International Book Award Finalist. How do you feel these accolades have impacted your writing career and your mission to share the good news through your books?

It is hard to determine if the awards have much impact on my career, but I do feel receiving awards might bring credibility to my writing. Perhaps parents, teachers, or librarians might be more inclined to read a book that has had an award.

Assessing Learners with Special Needs: An Applied Approach is a practical guide for educators. How do you see your expertise in educational psychology intersecting with your passion for writing Christian fiction and devotionals?

My writing is geared to teaching as it was in the assessment textbook. In the future, I will be offering study guides for some of the Christian books for children.

Unveiling the Mind's Revolution

JOHAN COOLS

Exploring Cognitive Health, Societal Transformation, and the Path to Collective Enlightenment

Johan Cools delves into his visionary work, addressing the Brain Pandemic, offering tools for transformation, and envisioning a harmonious society through cognitive evolution.

Hailing from the picturesque city of Gent, Belgium, Johan Cools emerges as a luminary in the realms of cognitive health, mental transformation, and societal evolution. Born in Belgium, Cools embarked on a profound journey intersecting diverse fields—from cancer and health research to the exploration of natural healing and vibrational medicine. However, it is his relentless pursuit of understanding the human psyche, neuroplasticity, and the subconscious mind that sets him apart as a visionary in the modern era.

Cools' odyssey into the intricacies of cognitive well-being culminated in the creation of transformative literary works, poised to revolutionize how we perceive and nurture our mental faculties. As the curtains unveil on his upcoming masterpiece, 'Modern Lifestyle Kills,' slated for release in 2024, readers are invited to embark on a voyage of self-discovery and societal rejuvenation.

Central to Cools' discourse is the ground-breaking concept of the "Brain Pandemic," a poignant metaphor illuminating the pervasive cognitive crisis gripping humanity. Drawing parallels to the urgency witnessed in medical pandemics, Cools advocates for a collective awakening to the imperative of mental well-being. Through his profound insights, he unveils a roadmap for personal and societal transformation, offering practical tools and methodologies to navigate the tumultuous landscape of the modern mind.

Embedded within the fabric of his narrative are the endearing characters of the cartoon family The Knewits, , serving as beacons of wisdom in a sea of complexity. Through their trials and triumphs, readers are beckoned to confront their own cognitive landscapes, fostering empathy, understanding, and resilience along the way.

Yet, Cools' vision extends far beyond individual enlightenment, resonating with the pulse of a harmonious society. At its core lies a call to action—a call to embrace empathy, collaboration, and social responsibility. Through the synergy of hearts and minds, he envisions a world where authenticity reigns supreme, and humanity thrives in interconnectedness.

As readers delve into the pages of Cools' magnum opus, they are not merely passive spectators but active participants in a profound paradigm shift—one that transcends the boundaries of the self and ushers in an era of collective evolution. With every turn of the page, a symphony of transformation unfolds, echoing the resounding truth that within each individual lies the power to reshape not only their reality but the fabric of society itself.

How did you come up with the

concept of a Brain pandemic and what inspired you to address this topic in your book?

The term Brain Pandemic suggests a widespread cognitive health crisis necessitating urgent action, akin to the global mobilization seen in medical pandemics. It serves as a metaphor for pervasive mental challenges, highlighting the importance of mental well-being and the transformation of thought processes. By evoking the recent COVID-19 experience, I intended to create cultural resonance, emphasizing the danger of passive conformism and learnt helplessness, while epxressing the need for a collective, transformative response to the real challenges humanity and our society is facing by enhancing cognitive functioning.

Can you elaborate on the practical tools and methods you provide in the book for personal and societal transformation?

This book offers the readers techniques to recognize and restructure habitual thought patterns that operate beneath conscious awareness. Moving beyond the confines of routine thinking is facilitated by the concept of the 6E ORBIT, which encourages stepping out of one's mental comfort zone and dispelling the illusions created by virtual reality. To cleanse the subconscious mind, I introduce Mental Transformation Animations (MTAs), which leverage a blend of visualizations, affirmations,

> *Johan Cools' visionary insights illuminate paths to personal growth and societal harmony, forging a brighter future through cognitive revolution.*

and meditation technologies, such as BrainTap, to rewire mental pathways. For those seeking heightened productivity and perfor-

mance, there is a chapter about the importance of the heart and flow state—a zone of peak engagement and focus. Communication skills are also addressed, offering a comprehensive guide to enhance interpersonal connections, particularly when sharing critical or controversial information. Lastly, the book fosters critical thinking through the "Fake News Questionnaire," a tool designed to help readers discern the reliability in an information landscape controlled and censured by mass media.

What motivated you to incorporate the characters of The Knewits in your book, and how do they contribute to the narrative?

The Knewits add a narrative layer, making complex ideas more accessible and engaging by giving readers characters to relate to and learn from. Through the family's experiences, the book's concepts are vividly demonstrated in real-life scenarios, enhancing reader engagement and making the material more enjoyable and memorable. Readers often form an emotional bond with the characters, which can increase their motivation to integrate the book's lessons into their own lives. Furthermore, the storytelling approach aids memory retention, as the Knewit cartoons can act as mnemonic devices for recalling key points. The insights that the family members experience or the challenges they face underscore the messages of personal growth. Light-heartedness and humour in the narrative help to soften the delivery of serious content, while the diverse viewpoints within the family reflect a range of controversial perspectives, emphasizing the need for an open mind.

How do you suggest individuals can effectively apply the principles discussed in the book to their daily lives for tangible results?

Firstly it's essential to set inten-

tions that extend beyond the self and foster deeper connections with others. This starts with finding back your authentic self and connection with yourself. Then you set goals that reflect a commitment to broader societal engagement. Small, intentional actions can gradually expand your circle of positive influence, fostering the confidence to enact more significant transformations. Mindfulness and an open mind become crucial, not just for self-awareness but also for discerning the impact of external influences, such as the fear mongering mass media and the pressure of societal conformism. By integrating these principles and insights into your daily life, you cultivate habits that counteract the narrow focus of self-centeredness. The tools provided in this book should be used while keeping your intentions aligned with a greater purpose of contribution, and not limited to personal progress. It is also important to keep educating yourself with an open mind by seeking out authentic sources of information that challenge false narratives. Within these processes patience and persistence are important because societal change and personal change unfold gradually. Finally, it's important to celebrate not only personal milestones but also the small or bigger accomplished changes which contribute towards a loss polar, more connected and empathic world.

What do you hope readers will take away from the book in terms of enhancing their cognitive abilities and contributing to a more harmonious society?

In terms of enhancing cognitive abilities, this book aims to empower readers with a mindset geared towards continuous learning, by applying metathinking and stepping out of their comfort zone. By reflecting on the way thoughts and emotions create your reality you gain the power to reshape

your reality. So I encourage the development of critical thinking, a crucial skill in discerning truth in an age of mass media manipulation. Mindfulness is presented as a tool for increasing self-awareness and managing cognitive biases. If the reader understands neuroplasticity then they have a tool to reshape their limiting beliefs, their lives and their reality. The idea is to empower the reader and to bring them the insight that they are not a helpless drop on a hot plate, but a drop in a powerful wave of increased consciousness that can transform society in a more human friendly direction.

For contributing to a more harmonious society, the book underscores the importance of empathy in recognizing and valuing diverse perspectives, leading to more compassionate interactions. It also stresses the significance of effective communication, enabling individuals to share ideas and listen to understand, which is essential for creating trust. Collaboration is key, as many societal challenges are best addressed through united efforts. A sense of social responsibility is encouraged, emphasizing the impact of individual contributions to the community. The book promotes global awareness, recognizing the interconnectedness and interdependence of all living creatures in our ecosystem and a new way of thinking using the brain-heart to compensate for a left brain dominated technocratic society which is leading to degeneration and regression of humanity to digital slavery.

Crafting Realms with
MICHAEL ALAN PECK
Exploring the Intricate World of 'The Commons' and the Power of Imagination

Michael Peck discusses inspiration, character development, and themes in "The Commons," weaving tales of surreal landscapes, complex characters, and profound messages.

In the vivid tapestry of storytelling, Michael Peck stands as both weaver and architect, crafting realms where imagination reigns supreme. With a career spanning the worlds of television, travel, and gastronomy, Peck has honed his craft with the written word as his guiding star, infusing each narrative with humor, depth, and a touch of the surreal.

Peck's latest venture, The Commons, unfolds as a labyrinthine landscape where the ordinary collides with the extraordinary, and the mundane transforms into the miraculous. In a recent interview with Reader's House Magazine, he delves into the genesis of this intricate universe, tracing its roots to childhood influences like the Krofft brothers' fantastical creations and the literary realms crafted by Stan Lee and Stephen King.

Central to The Commons is its diverse cast of characters, each bearing complexities that mirror the human condition. From the streetwise Paul to the enigmatic mythicals like Po and Ken, Peck deftly navigates tropes and expectations, imbuing his creations with depth and nuance that defy convention.

At the heart of this sprawling narrative stands the chilling figure of Mr. Brill, a corporate raider whose grip on the afterlife serves as a potent allegory for unchecked greed and the erosion of empathy. Through Brill and his ilk, Peck probes the depths of human nature, exploring themes of redemption, sacrifice, and the enduring power of hope.

Journeying through The Commons unveils a phantasmagoria of surreal landscapes and whimsical creatures, a testament to Peck's boundless imagination and the influence of luminaries like Neil Gaiman. Here, rules bend and reality wavers, inviting readers into a realm where the extraordinary is rendered ordinary and the mundane takes on new meaning.

Yet amidst the fantastical flourishes, The Journeyman also grapples with profound questions of unseen potential and the essence of humanity. Through characters like Zach, Peck shines a light on the transformative power of choice, reminding us that within each individual lies the capacity for both greatness and goodness.

As readers embark on this odyssey through The Commons, they are invited to ponder their own role in shaping the world around them. For in Peck's universe, it is not the grandeur of realms or the majesty of creatures that defines greatness, but rather the choices we make and the depths of compassion we are willing to explore.

What inspired you to create the intricate world of The Commons, and how did you approach building its unique mythology?

I've always been fascinated by the idea of being trapped in an alien world. I suppose I'd have to blame the Krofft brothers because I grew up on '70s American Saturday-morning fare such as H.R. Pufnstuf, Lidsville, and Land of the Lost, which all involved a kid or a family from our world ending up in a strange land they couldn't escape. And I was drawn into just how weird it was. I mean, you're stuck with a bunch of talking hats because you fell into one?

I'd also hold Stan Lee and Stephen King responsible because I moved on to more intricate, more dangerous worlds as I grew up reading Marvel comics and King's novels. And I thought that layering on a world drawn from the imaginings, dreams, and nightmares of everyone who's ever passed through it made it even more interesting.

As far as its mythology goes, I wanted it to look like something that emerged from chaos and created its own sort of order (as much as there is one) out of necessity. It was never supposed to be the world that it became. The dead—"real" people, or bona fides in the lingo of The Commons— were meant to move through it to determine their ultimate destination. They were supposed to take their Essence—or life force—with them when they went. And the mythicals—the imagined beings and entities from the bona fides' former lives—should have disappeared once those who created them moved on. When Mr. Brill took over and started stealing all of the Essence for himself, the works got gummed up, so to speak.

What does a world that wasn't meant to have such a population look like when it's filled with made-up creatures and beings that can't move on? That's what I set out to build.

The characters in "The Journeyman" are diverse and complex. Can you share your process for developing their personalities and arcs?

Mainly, I wanted to explore what happens when you take a certain trope or expected type of character and put them into a situation outside of the story they're supposed to live in. Paul is a street kid whose life has been about determination in the face of helplessness. He's never had much, and now suddenly he's potentially one of the most powerful beings in this world he's landed in. But he doesn't know how to use that power and isn't sure what he's supposed to do with it.

The mythicals are standard types who become their own type of being when they're allowed to go their own way. Po is a shaolin monk who's angry because he's a stereotype from an old kung-fu movie. So he has a temper. And he doesn't speak because his voice is an offensive cliche, which he can't help. Ken is a monster, outwardly, but is one of the kindest and most philosophical of the characters. Zach is a special-needs kid who's a lot stronger than he appears to be. And so on. I wanted to take conventions we think we know and turn them on their head a bit. I'm three books in, and they have a lot more surprises in them to come.

The concept of Mr. Brill as a corporate raider controlling the afterlife is both fascinating and chilling. What inspired this antagonist, and what message or themes were you exploring through his character?

Mr. Brill and the antagonists who succeed him are toxic corporatism personified. You see him in the real world. Greedy and powerful types who justify taking everything for themselves by trying to tell everyone that's the natural way of things, ie: it's your job to grab all you can. And if you end up on the wrong end of the equation, it's your fault. You weren't strong enough or good enough at the game.

Brill is what happens when we ignore our empathy and generosity. Or, worse, when we let it curdle and transform into the opposite of what it's supposed to be, where we blame those who suffer in such a system. We know the difference between right and wrong. We just have to remember it—and want to.

The novel explores themes of redemption, sacrifice, and the power of hope. What message or takeaway do you hope readers will gain from these themes?

You have more power than you think you do. They need you to believe you don't. They want you to think the decisions should all be left up to them because they're better and smarter than you. That's why they have all the money, right? Because they deserve it, and you don't. Nonsense. We have hope and love. And hope and love are power.

The journey through The Commons is filled with surreal landscapes and imaginative creatures. How did you go about crafting these fantastical elements, and were there any particular influences or inspirations?

If I had to choose one strong influence, it would be Neil Gaiman's Sandman comics. I wanted The Commons to feel much like an American version of The Dreaming. A fantastic landscape should resonate like a dream does—as something very strange and dynamic, with weird combinations of landscapes, inhabitants and objects. And things can change at any time. The strange and ridiculous can have weight, meaning, and poignance, and what seems to be important and momentous in the waking world easily fades away in this imaginary place.

There are rules, but they change, and they don't necessarily match the rules we're used to in the "real" world.

The Journeyman touches on the idea of unseen potential and the depths of human capability, particularly through characters like Zach. What motivated you to incorporate this aspect into the story, and what significance does it hold for you personally?

Ultimately, human capability is the most we have to offer. It's a double-edged sword, of course. We can use that capability to destroy each other, our home, ourselves. Or we can bring it to bear in order to help one another and build ourselves up by building everyone up. It's all a matter of what motivates you. Do you want to use that capability to further only your own ends, even if it's at everyone else's expense? Or do you want to use it for good? In the end, it's people choosing to do the right thing, to help one another, even at great cost to themselves. Selfishness is an easy choice because so many people are doing it. Sacrifice for the greater good is hard. That's why so few people choose it.

The Multifaceted Journey of

BRAD BALUKJIAN

Exploring Truth, Humanity, and the Unconventional in Science, Journalism, and Literature

In the realm where journalism and science intersect, Brad Balukjian, PhD stands as a dynamic figure, his pursuits weaving a tapestry of curiosity, truth-seeking, and storytelling. A published author whose bylines grace the pages of esteemed publications like Rolling Stone, Smithsonian, and National Geographic, Balukjian's multidisciplinary journey spans from the halls of academia to the open road. His debut book, *The Wax Pack: On the Open Road in Search of Baseball's Afterlife*, not only ascended to the ranks of the LA Times bestseller list but also earned recognition as one of NPR's Best Books of 2020. Yet, his narrative prowess doesn't solely rest within the confines of literary acclaim; as a Research Associate at the California Academy of Sciences, he's unveiled the secrets of Tahitian insects, even immortalizing Harrison Ford in the taxonomy of entomology.

Embarking on odysseys that transcend the conventional, Balukjian's works serve as portals into realms both familiar and obscure. From the hallowed grounds of baseball to the squared circle of professional wrestling, he traverses landscapes of nostalgia, loss, and personal discovery, extracting narratives that resonate with the universal human experience. In a conversation with Reader's House Magazine, Balukjian offers insights into his unconventional approach to storytelling, the symbiosis between his scientific and literary endeavors, and the profound connections that thread through his narratives.

From his childhood passions to the corridors of academia, Balukjian's journey is one of relentless pursuit—a quest to uncover truths, unveil hidden narratives, and bridge the chasm between hero and human. As readers delve into his works, they're invited not only to witness the lives of icons but also to confront the echoes of their own stories reflected in the pages. Balukjian's oeuvre stands as a testament to the transformative power of storytelling, a beacon guiding aspiring writers to embrace the unconventional, traverse the uncharted, and unearth the profound in the overlooked.

What inspired you to embark on journeys that led to writing books like *The Six Pack* and *The Wax Pack*?

I was trained as a magazine journalist in the craft of longform narrative journalism (a craft that is becoming increasingly rare, unfortunately), and always dreamed of being able to flex those muscles in the space afforded by a book. I loved four things when I was a kid--baseball, wrestling, islands, and Star Wars--and still love those four things to this day. With baseball and wrestling, it wasn't enough for me to have my heroes, I wanted to know everything about them, to know what they are like as people beyond the performance on the field or in the ring. I have a somewhat obsessive nature (and truly have OCD, as documented in The Wax Pack), which comes in handy when you're doing a PhD on Tahitian insects or writing a book about former athletes. Embarking on these road trips to track down the heroes of my youth gave me the opportunity to indulge that childhood passion while also attempting to paint portraits of the humanity of these people who experienced a level of fame you and I will never know.

Brad Balukjian, scientist and journalist, delves into his journeys behind "The Six Pack" and "The Wax Pack," intertwining nostalgia, discovery, and human connection

How did your background in island biogeography and entomology inform your approach to storytelling in your books?

There is surprising and substantial overlap between my two career choices, science and journalism. Both are about seeking truth through the compilation of evidence to test some hypothesis and answer some question about the world. With my entomology research I started with the question of: how many species of green flash bugs are there on these islands? With The Six Pack it was, to what extent did each of these wrestlers become their character? That's why the title of each chapter pits the wrestler against himself, e.g. Terry Bollea vs. Hulk Hogan. Terry Bollea is a sensitive kid from Port Tampa, Florida while Hulk Hogan is the paragon of virtue from Venice Beach, California.

Can you share an anecdote from your travels that particularly resonated with you or shaped your perspective on the subjects you were exploring?

One of the wrestlers in The Six Pack who I covered is named Tony Atlas (real name: Anthony White). Tony, who is Black, grew up in abject poverty in western Virginia in the 1950s and 1960s, a time when overt racism dominated the South as Jim Crow was still very much in effect. Not only did Tony have to contend with that, he was placed in a boys home during his adolescence, where he told me he had to fight all the time to not get raped. Before he was 18, Tony had already dealt with more adversity than most people experience in a lifetime, and so to see him rise out of that to become a star and then crash and burn due to having too much too soon was powerful stuff. I wanted to see his hometown for myself, so I drove to Low Moor, Virginia, and creeping around those country roads at ten miles per hour I got a true appreciation for the place that shaped him. Place matters in books like these, and I wanted to be able to describe that place first-hand.

In The Six Pack, you delve into the lives of professional wrestlers from the 1980s. What drew you to this particular era and subculture within wrestling?

The mid-to-late 1980s WWF was a unique period in wrestling history because of the extreme schedule that was kept. The WWF put on almost 1,000 shows per year, with three troupes running in different parts of the country, with no off-season. Many of these wrestlers performed 310-320 days per year, with a flight every day to a new city. Sure wrestling is staged, but having gotten in the ring myself for a day of training, I can tell you that that canvas is no trampoline, and these guys took a beating. They had no health insurance, no union, no retirement plan. If they didn't wrestle, they didn't get paid. What does that do to a person? To their psyche? To their family?

The Wax Pack takes a unique approach by tracing the lives of baseball players from a single pack of cards. What challenges did you face in tracking down these players, and were there any unexpected revelations during your journey?

Delve into the lives of 1980s wrestling icons with Brad Balukjian's "The Six Pack," a journey of resilience, fame, and humanity.

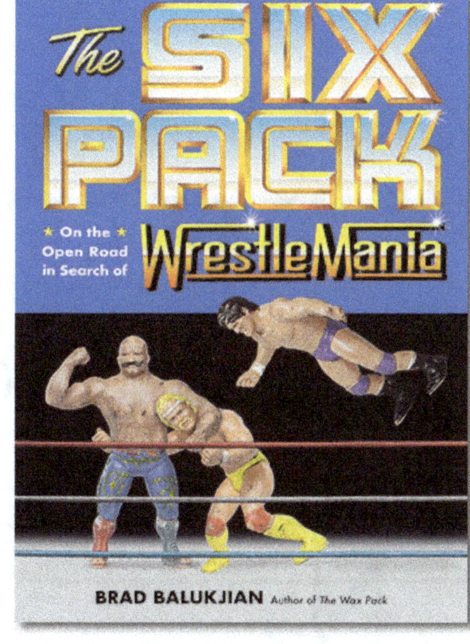

I consider myself first and foremost a travel writer. I take the reader on the road with me to investigate the afterlives of our childhood heroes. I'm not a baseball or sportswriter, and I don't have the pedigree in those areas that might impress a potential interview subject. So it was challenging to get some of the former players to talk to me because they may not have felt it was worth their time. That book produced plenty of surprises. For example, when I set out I had no idea what a pivotal role the father/son relationship would play in that story. And not just the feel-good Field of Dreams father-son stuff, but the dark side as well.

Both of your books explore themes of nostalgia, loss, and personal discovery. How do you navigate these themes while maintaining an engaging narrative for your readers?

These are universal themes that we can all relate to, which is why I write these books with a general reader in mind. You don't have to be a baseball or wrestling fan to enjoy these books. I think that teasing out these themes is what helps make the narrative engaging, because the reader is hopefully emotionally invested. I also try to draw on the techniques of the New Journalism (dialogue, point-of-view, status-conveying details) to paint a vivid picture of the scenes that I am in.

Your books seem to blend elements of memoir, investigative journalism, and travelogue. How do you balance these different storytelling modes, and what do you hope readers take away from your work?

I try to write books similar to those I most enjoy reading, which is narrative non-fiction where the reader is informed, entertained, and emotionally engaged. By combining these different genres, I believe the widest set of potential readers is served. But it's a tightrope walk because go too far in one direction and you'll lose your audience. I hope readers take away how much they have in common with their heroes. These baseball players and athletes are people just like you and me, and they contend with the same challenges in life that we contend with. Everything in life is tradeoffs.

What advice would you give to aspiring writers who are interested in pursuing unconventional storytelling formats or exploring niche subcultures in their work?

Don't rush it, take the time to understand your subject matter at a deep level. Be willing to take risks and stick to your convictions, but at the same time be wary of expectations. The road of suffering is paved in expectation. Be honest about your motivation for a particular project and adjust your goals accordingly. Are you writing this to make money? For creative fulfilment? Be honest.

Brad Balukjian's multidisciplinary approach illuminates hidden narratives, bridging science and storytelling with grace, depth, and universal resonance.

MARCI GREENBERG COX

Navigating Cancer Diagnosis and Parenthood with Grace and Resilience

Navigating the turbulent waters of a cancer diagnosis is a daunting journey, one fraught with uncertainty, fear, and numerous challenges. For Marci Greenberg Cox, this journey became a defining chapter in her life, igniting a passion for advocacy and support that reverberates through her work today. In 2018, Marci found herself confronted with a Stage 3 breast cancer diagnosis, thrust into a world of surgeries, chemotherapy, and the emotional turmoil of explaining her illness to her young daughters.

In the face of adversity, Marci's resilience shone brightly. Rather than succumbing to despair, she embraced open dialogue with her children, crafting a narrative of hope and understanding amidst the chaos. This experience sparked the genesis of "Mommy Has a Boo-Boo," a poignant tale born from her own struggles, aimed at helping families navigate the complexities of cancer diagnoses with grace and honesty.

But Marci's journey didn't end there. Fueled by a desire to support others facing similar challenges, she embarked on a literary endeavor, penning additional books and journals to offer guidance and solace to those in need. Her creation of Flor Publishing in 2020 further solidified her commitment to providing resources and a sense of community for individuals and families affected by cancer.

In a recent interview with Reader's House Magazine, Marci delved into the inspiration behind her writing, the personal journey that influenced her work, and the profound impact her books have had on readers facing similar battles. Through candid discussions and heartfelt reflections, she shares not only her experiences but also invaluable advice for parents and caregivers navigating the delicate task of discussing cancer with young children.

Marci's dedication to advocacy knows no bounds. With future projects aimed at expanding her literary repertoire to include diverse representations and themes, she remains steadfast in her mission to empower and uplift those affected by cancer, offering a beacon of hope in the darkest of times. Through her website and publications, she continues to weave a tapestry of resilience and courage, reminding us all that in the face of adversity, there is always strength to be found.

What inspired you to write "Mommy Has a Boo-Boo"?

In November 2018, my life took an unexpected turn when I was diagnosed with Stage 3 Breast Cancer—a journey that would test my strength and resilience in ways I never imagined. As I grappled with the reality of my diagnosis, one of my greatest challenges was finding the right words to explain it to my young daughters, then aged 5 and 1, as well as to my 15-year-old stepdaughter.

How did your personal journey with breast cancer influence the writing process?

Throughout my aggressive treatment regimen, including a double mastectomy and chemotherapy, I was determined to maintain open communication with my children, ensuring they understood my illness without feeling overwhelmed by fear of losing me. This experience inspired me to pen my first book, "Mommy Has a Boo-Boo," a heartfelt account of my journey and a guide for other families facing similar challenges.

However, my eldest daughter, still curious and uneasy about my appearance without hair, prompted me to create another resource. Thus, "Mommy Has a Boo-Boo Now What?" was born—a journal designed to facilitate discussions between parents and children, addressing their concerns and fostering understanding and support.

Reflecting on my own initial confusion and anxiety upon diagnosis, I recognized the need for a comprehensive guide to navigating the complexities of breast cancer. This led me to author "The Breast Cancer GPS," a practical handbook offering insights into medical procedures, questions for healthcare professionals, and coping strategies for those confronting the unknown.

The response from both the medical community and women battling breast cancer has been overwhelming. The necessity for these books is palpable. While I didn't receive formal feedback on these three particular books, they stem from my personal journey and reflections during that time.

What advice would you give to parents or caregivers who need to discuss cancer with young children?

I consistently advocate for honesty and openness between mothers and their children when facing illness. Children have an innate sense that something is amiss, and skirting around the issue isn't fair to them. Contrary to what we might assume, children demonstrate remarkable resilience. Naturally, the approach varies depending on their age, but honesty remains paramount when explaining to them that "mommy has a boo-boo."

Moreover, I'm fervently passionate about advocating for the rights of younger women to access proper medical care. Despite the standard recommendation in the US for mammograms starting at 40, there's a growing population of women in their 20s and 30s receiving diagnoses. It's unjust that insurance dictates when a woman can seek preventive care.

What future projects or initiatives do you have in mind to continue supporting individuals and families affected by breast cancer or cancer in general?

My latest releases, "Michael the Magnificent Fights Back" and "Maggie the Magnificent Fights Back," tackle the challenging theme of children confronting a cancer diagnosis. I aim to expand this series to encompass eight books featuring diverse characters. While the current editions focus on Caucasian characters, I'm committed to creating representations of African American, Asian, and Indian characters. Cancer knows no boundaries, and it's essential for children to see themselves reflected in these narratives.

Today, I continue to share my journey and insights through my website, www.florpublishing. com, and my books are available on Amazon. My mission is to empower and support individuals and families facing similar challenges, providing them with the tools and resources they need to navigate their own journeys with courage and resilience.

Mommy Has a Boo-Boo beautifully explains breast cancer to children, fostering understanding and hope through simple language and heartfelt illustrations.

Mommy Has a Boo-Boo: Explaining Breast Cancer to Children by Marci Greenberg Cox, with contributions from Kristen Hampshire and Brooke Foster, is a touching and invaluable resource for families navigating the challenging journey of a breast cancer diagnosis. Aimed at children aged 3-9, this book gently introduces the concept of cancer in a way that is both accessible and comforting.

The narrative follows a mother's experience with breast cancer, covering key events such as surgery, chemotherapy, and the physical changes that come with treatment. Through simple, clear language and engaging illustrations, children can better understand why their mommy might look different and what she is going through. The story is both honest and hopeful, emphasizing that while the journey is tough, recovery and healing are possible.

Readers have praised the book for its effectiveness in sparking important conversations between parents and children. One parent noted that it provides a "perfectly sweet, simple way to describe to your young child exactly what is to come," while another highlighted its educational value in explaining cancer and its impact on the family.

The book is a heartfelt, educational tool that supports families during a difficult time. It reassures young readers that even though their mommy has a "*boo-boo*" called cancer, with time and care, she will get better. This book is highly recommended for any family facing breast cancer, offering a sense of understanding and hope for both children and parents.

TRISTAN ZELDEN

From Entertainment Journalism to Fiction Writing: Exploring the Genesis of 'The Huntress and the Trickster'

Tristan Zelden, a former entertainment journalist with a penchant for delving into the worlds of video games, movies, and television, brings his storytelling prowess to the forefront in his debut novel, *The Huntress and the Trickster.* A graduate of California State University, Fullerton, with a degree in journalism, Zelden's transition from reporting on the fantastical to crafting it himself speaks volumes about his passion for narrative.

In this exclusive interview with Reader's House Magazine, Zelden shares insights into his creative process, revealing the inspirations and challenges behind the fusion of urban fantasy and thriller that defines his novel. Rooted in a love for the likes of *John Wick* and the recent *God of War* games, Zelden's narrative concoction emerges from the collision of these two worlds, sparking the inception of a tale where a John Wick-esque assassin crosses paths with Norse gods.

Zelden's journalistic background permeates his approach to fiction, as he seamlessly weaves research and storytelling to construct a world both believable and captivating. Through the lens of Abigail Byrne, a formidable yet conflicted protagonist, Zelden explores themes of workaholism and personal sacrifice, grounding his narrative in the complexities of human relationships amidst a backdrop of danger and intrigue.

The Huntress and the Trickster is not merely a tale of action and mythology; it is a testament to Zelden's meticulous world-building, where the mundane and the magical coalesce to form a tapestry of rich narrative tapestry. From the intricacies of assassin culture to the nuances of Norse mythology, Zelden's attention to detail lends authenticity to his storytelling, inviting readers to immerse themselves fully in his fictional universe.

As Zelden reflects on his journey from journalism to fiction writing, he offers valuable insights and advice to aspiring authors navigating the daunting landscape of publishing. From staying true to one's creative vision to embracing the learning curve of the publishing process, Zelden's wisdom serves as a guiding light for those embarking on their own literary endeavors.

In an age where the boundaries between literature and other forms of media blur, Zelden's narrative prowess stands as a testament to the enduring power of storytelling. Through *The Huntress and the Trickster,* he invites readers on a thrilling journey that transcends genres and captivates the imagination—an invitation not to be missed.

Tristan Zelden is a former entertainment journalist who covered video games, movies, and TV. Graduating from California State University, Fullerton, he got his Bachelor's degree in journalism and a passion to start writing. He currently is focused on his career as a novelist with the hope of getting horror novels published. While working on future novels, he tends to read, play video games, get tattoos, and look at cute pictures of dogs and bears on social media.

Your debut novel, *The Huntress and the Trickster,* blends elements of urban fantasy with a thriller narrative. What inspired you to combine these genres, and how did you approach creating a unique world and story within them?

The idea all came from two different worlds. I

Tristan Zelden discusses inspirations, world-building, and the journey from journalism to fiction in crafting his debut novel, blending urban fantasy with thriller elements.

am a huge fan of John Wick and the last two God of War games. I did a rewatch of the first three, at the time only, John Wick movies. Around that time, I replayed 2018's God of War entry. Consuming two things I love dearly popped up this idea in my head that made me think, *"What if a John Wick-like assassin went up against a Norse god?"* From there, I went into world-building, character development, and building out this story. It all came rather naturally as I thought about the idea for months to years before ever writing it. When I did finally commit, I did my research and took notes to figure out the characters and world. Much of that world-building and character development came from making it as grounded as possible despite the fantastical elements. What would the world be like if assassins were legalized workers? How do Norse gods fit into the universe? I asked myself many questions about logic, legality, and lore to create a believable and captivating world.

As a journalist covering video games, movies, and TV, how has your experience in

media influenced your approach to writing fiction? Are there any specific lessons or skills from journalism that you found particularly valuable in crafting your novel?

The most obvious way journalism helped is the basic writing aspect of it all. It helped me refine my skills as a writer; although style, prose, and pretty much everything is different when writing fiction, I at least gained improvements in the foundation of writing. The other major skill I gained is research. As a journalist, I would ensure I had all the facts straight by researching. Other times, I would research to gain a better insight into the topic I was writing about. When writing fiction, I want it to be believable. So, I research all kinds of relevant topics to make my characters, world, and story come to life. I think covering so many topics when I was in journalism helped me get a broad view of things, especially when I was putting in the work to research all kinds of subjects.

Your protagonist, Abigail Byrne, is described as a workaholic assassin caught up in a dangerous job. What inspired the creation of this character, and what challenges did you face in developing her personality and motivations throughout the story?

The story was intended, thematically, to be about workaholics and how consuming work culture is. Abigail has a great relationship with her husband, Jacob. Still, she creates her own friction because she is so devoted to working. The book shows the highs and lows of that relationship. That was probably the biggest challenge. I needed to balance the relationship she had with Jacob and her job, which the story attached itself to. These aspects are tied to her motivations, as she is determined to get this job done, but the pay could release her from her work enough to allow her to spend more time with Jacob. Will that actually get her to put in place some boundaries from work? It was aspects like that that made for a compelling character study. Striking that balance was tricky, but I think readers will get a great sense of her life, both professional and personal.

The creation of her came down to a few things. In the beginning, you get a great description of her.

She is big and muscular and tattooed all over. I love a good woman lead, especially in action. I find it inspiring and empowering but also different, as buff men take up too much of the zeitgeist. When I see these women in movies, they look great. They are fit and clearly trained, but there is an odd body standard that men must be muscular and women must be fit yet petite. Why can't the women be big and buff? I wanted to give that body representation because there are women who have those bodies and look great. I hope I nailed that because any woman reading the book who has muscles that are too big for society, I want them to see themselves and be proud of their lifestyle and body.

The Huntress and the Trickster features intricate world-building that blends grounded elements with fantastical elements. Can you tell us more about the process of building this fictional world, and were there any specific influences or inspirations that guided your world-building efforts?

There are two sides to the world-building, some of which I have already touched on. But for the assassin side, I had to think deeply about how it would be in real life. There are these different companies, like Hazardous, the one Abigail works for. How do those companies differentiate from one another? I love tattoos and incorporated that into the culture of assassins. They are mostly heavily tattooed people. In John Wick, you see some of that, and I loved that as a visual. The alternative, counter-culture aspect of it all gave my assassin world a personality. I thought about the legality of it all. How would this conflict with state laws in the U.S. versus federal? What restrictions would there be? Also, the corruption of it all. Power, money, and violence are all corrosive things. Sure, power and money can be used for good, but this book shows the evil of it. Abigail believes she is doing good, but not many people on the other end of her gun truly deserve to die. That is the corruption of it all. A world of violence devouring itself. So, there was that element of showcasing this in a political way but also in a compelling thriller story.

The other side is the Norse mythology element. I naturally have a fascination with Scandinavian culture and lore. The recent God of War games gave that interest a major boost. I also read Neil Gaiman's Norse Mythology. In that book, he has a few pages dedicated to the creative process. He talked about adhering to the mythology but taking influences from other people's stories and the fact that much of that part of history is gone. It is gone because of a mixture of factors, which leads to creative freedom. I wanted to make this believable so that when you get the explanation later on in the book, it comes together in a way that is digestible. Some of that explanation makes no sense because it is magical. Other parts feel real. I wanted to balance something that readers could have a firm grasp on, like the characters, but also feel just as confused as Abigail when navigating this fantastical element that shakes up a seemingly grounded world.

With your background in covering entertainment media, how do you see the relationship between literature and other forms of media evolving in the digital age? Do you believe that your experiences in journalism have influenced your approach to storytelling or marketing your novel?

I think all media is in this area that requires everyone to readjust themselves to figure out how to maintain sustainability. I am too new to the literary world to have a firm opinion, but from the data and studies I have read, I think it is in a good place. Literature is having a surplus of book sales and book stores opening in the pandemic era. Obviously, the pandemic was horrible, but some positives came out of it, like how the literary industry has been booming for the most part. I guess the big issue for all media is that there is so much, which makes for tough competition to get your work seen by an audience. But I won't complain. Lots of art is a great thing, whether it be film, video games, literature, or music.

I do think, for other kinds of media like video games and movies, it is in a tough space. It costs so much to make certain things that it makes it hard to profit. If it is hard to make a profit, the business people who make the decisions may skip out on what could be great art. It is about navigating the business and the art sides that make it difficult. I just hope people can figure out a way to make sustainable businesses that still let creatives make the things they want and maintain their truth as artists.

Journalism has influenced me to maintain authenticity. Now, it is less about reporting on facts and more about telling my truth. When I write fiction, I write what I find to be entertaining, thought-provoking, or emotionally evocative. I feel like I hadn't gained too much from journalism as a fiction author, but it has held me down to tell stories that I find to be important in one way or another.

What advice would you offer to aspiring authors who may be navigating the process of writing and publishing their first novel? Are there any lessons or insights from your own journey as an author that you believe would be helpful to share with others?

For the storytelling aspect of it all, tell stories you find entertaining. I can't remember the exact quote, but Stephen King said something along those lines about how he writes stories he finds entertaining. If you find the story entertaining, surely someone will find it entertaining, too. Just cross your fingers that the person is someone who can make things happen for you, like a literary agent or publisher.

My advice on the publishing side is to learn. Read about what other people have to say. Read about people's experiences. It is a complicated world that I am still figuring out myself. Take those chances and learn from them if it doesn't pan out. Life is all about taking action and then learning from the outcome, whether it is a win or loss. Just know that once you get your foot in the door, then some good will come out of it. Opportunities will, hopefully, come along. For me, I got to do interviews like this, which is great. Now that I have done something like this, maybe the right person will read it, and I can get another interview or another great opportunity.

Tristan Zelden crafts a mesmerizing fusion of urban fantasy and thriller, showcasing meticulous world-building and compelling character dynamics.

PHOTO: *Derek Borthwick, expert in sales and communication, shares his profound insights on mastering effective communication and personal development.*

Mastering Communication with

DEREK BORTHWICK

Unlocking the Secrets of Effective Communication

Derek Borthwick discusses overcoming communication challenges, mastering psychological techniques, and enhancing sales skills, offering practical tips and insights from his extensive experience and best-selling books.

Derek Borthwick stands out as a formidable expert in the field of communication, sales, and personal development. With over three decades of experience collaborating with some of the world's largest companies across Europe, Derek has honed his skills and insights into the human psyche, especially in the realm of sales and effective communication. He holds a plethora of qualifications, including a special honours degree in science, diplomas in business coaching, clinical hypnotherapy, and neuro-linguistic programming (NLP). Moreover, Derek is a certified Master Practitioner of NLP, bringing a wealth of knowledge to his practice.

In his prolific writing career, Derek has authored five influential books, such as *Inside The Mind Of Sales, Body Language: How To Read Anybody,* and *Public Speaking: How To Speak Effectively Without Fear, How To Eliminate Negative Thinking* and *How To Talk To Anybody.* Each of his books delves deep into understanding human behaviour and offers practical techniques to enhance communication skills and overcome psychological barriers. His upcoming book promises to add yet another valuable resource to his extensive body of work.

In our interview, Derek sheds light on the common challenges people face in communication, from overcoming nervousness in business situations to mastering the art of making others feel valued and heard. He emphasizes the importance of controlling one's state of mind and being aware of psychological biases that influence our interactions. Derek shares actionable techniques, such as the power of nonverbal cues and the strategic use of language, which readers can start applying immediately to improve their communication skills.

Derek's unique approach, encapsulated in his Power2Mind program, integrates both conscious and unconscious learning. By targeting the emotional brain through repetition, imagery, and emotion, Derek's methods ensure a holistic and profound transformation. His success stories, including remarkable personal transformations, attest to the efficacy of his techniques.

Join us as we explore Derek Borthwick's insights and discover how to unlock your potential in communication and beyond.

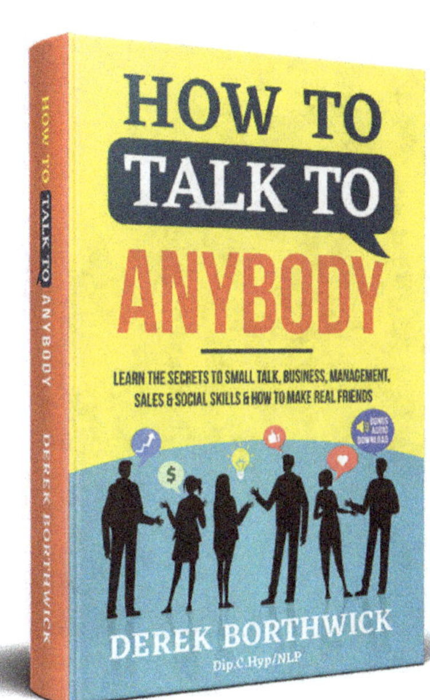

How to Talk to Anybody by Derek Borthwick is an exceptional guide that profoundly enhances communication skills, offering invaluable insights into human behavior and motivation, while providing practical techniques that are applicable in a myriad of social and professional contexts.

What are the biggest challenges that people face when communicating with others?

Many people feel uncomfortable speaking in business situations or when speaking to strangers They worry about making a fool of themselves, not knowing what to say and feel nervous. If not addressed, this can develop into a "runaway panic state", and the neocortex or thinking brain shuts down which compounds the problem.

How can we control our state to help us communicate better?

If you don't control your state than someone else or something else will do it for you. Remember nobody makes you nervous, you do this to yourself by choosing how you to react to a situation. There are many techniques to control your state both consciously and unconsciously, one of which are my specialist "rapid learning accelerator" audio programmes that specifically target the unconscious mind to assist with this.

What are some of the psychological biases that we should be aware of?

The first thing to realise is that while everyone is different, it turns out "just not that different". For example, everyone likes to feel important and valued. People like to feel as if somebody is listening and interested in what they are saying. People won't remember what you said but they will remember how you made them feel. If you want to be seen as more interesting, then be more interested. People resist what they are told and accept what they conclude. They are more likely to comply if you give them a reason. It does not have to be 100% accurate just plausible.

Are there some techniques things that you can share with the readers that they can start using immediately?

The first thing to realise is that people are remarkably self-centred. Think about a photograph of you and a group of your friends, when you see the picture who do you look at first? At this point most people have a wry smile. Everyone is tuned to a radio station "WIIFM" which stands for "what's in it for me". You must address what it is in it for somebody when you are speaking to them.

It is important when we are communicating with people that we show that we are listening too. One of the ways that we can do this is nonverbally, by tilting our head to one side at a 20° angle, and nod occasionally. This unconscious signal shows somebody that you are interested in what they're saying.

When speaking never use "but" as this negates what they have just said. "I hear what you are saying….. but". Use "and" instead as linguistically this joins two thoughts and does negate part of a sentence.

Could you give an example of a particularly impactful transformation you've witnessed in someone who has applied your techniques?

I've worked with a young individual where the results were miraculous. Initially he could not speak in public and had no confidence. We worked on both conscious and unconscious learning (using the audio programs). His sales improved, he entered a relationship and became the top salesperson. Recently he sent me a video by message and I had to do a "double-take" as I didn't realise that it was him at first such was the transformation. He was unrecognisable from the quivering wreck that I first encountered.

What sets your approach apart from other coaching and training programs, especially those focused on communication and influence?

Power2Mind targets both conscious and unconscious learning. There are four pillars to success (BSRA)

- Belief
- State Control
- Rapport
- Awareness

Power2Mind is based upon those pillars.

If you ask a professional sportsperson to explain what they do, they won't be able to because they do it unconsciously. We must target both the unconscious and the conscious mind and the emotional brain. The unconscious respond to repetition, imagery and emotion. Power2Mind uses special techniques and audio programs to do this together and incorporates an emotional understanding. That's the secret.

Why are you books different?

The first half of the books show how people are wired, and aim to get you thinking and to question certain pre-existing beliefs and assumptions. The second part of the books show a step-by-step approach to developing the skills. All books come with a complimentary audio that targets the unconscious mind to speed up the learning process. This means that we are using a multi pronged approach to gaining the skill.

Journey of Illumination

CHRISTOPHER LINK

From Personal Struggle to Spiritual Enlightenment

Christopher Link shares his journey from adversity to authorship, discussing spiritual awakening, defining true reality, and aspirations to guide others toward enlightenment.

Embarking on a journey from the depths of personal struggle to the radiant shores of spiritual enlightenment, Christopher Link's story is one of profound transformation. At 50, residing in the vibrant heart of Las Vegas, Nevada, Link stands as a beacon of inspiration, his newly published book shining brightly as a testament to his unwavering dedication to uplift others on their spiritual journeys.

In his interview with Reader's House Magazine, Link candidly shares the intricate tapestry of his life experiences that have woven together to form the fabric of his mission today. From the trials of a challenging childhood to the triumph of becoming a successful author and spiritual teacher, his narrative resonates with authenticity and resilience. Link's passion for creative writing and spiritual teaching, coupled with his aspirations to become a Spiritual Life Coach and his love for music as a drummer, reflects a multifaceted soul driven by a desire to serve others.

Link's debut book, "Coming Out of the Illusion: Realizing the Real You," delves deep into themes of self-discovery and liberation from societal constructs. Rooted in his own journey of awakening, the book serves as a guiding light for those navigating the labyrinth of existence. With each chapter meticulously crafted from his own spiritual growth and self-realization, Link offers invaluable insights gleaned from the crucible of his personal struggles.

Central to Link's message is the invitation to break free from the shackles of illusion and embrace the truth that lies dormant within. His spiritual awakening, a radiant phoenix rising from the ashes of despair, catalyzed a profound shift in perspective, illuminating a path of self-empowerment and purpose.

Link's definition of true reality transcends the mundane existence of duality, beckoning seekers toward a higher consciousness imbued with love, compassion, and joy. Through his writing and teachings, he imparts invaluable wisdom, guiding individuals towards their own inner truth and higher self-awareness.

Discover the truth within. 'Coming Out of the Illusion: Realizing the Real You' guides readers on a journey of self-discovery.

Navigating the transition from a career in the flooring industry to that of a spiritual author and teacher has been a journey fraught with challenges and revelations. Yet, with unwavering perseverance and a steadfast commitment to his calling, Link continues to chart a course towards a future where his impact resonates far and wide.

As Link sets his sights on the horizon, his aspirations burn bright with the fervent hope of touching countless lives with his message of authenticity and empowerment. With the imminent release of his second book and a wealth of original content awaiting eager readers, Link stands poised on the precipice of a new chapter in his journey, ready to illuminate the path for all who seek the light of truth.

Your journey from a challenging childhood to becoming a successful author and spiritual teacher is truly inspiring. Can you share more about how your personal experiences shaped your path and led you to your current mission of assisting others in realizing their spiritual selves?

In my book I have chosen chapters such as Energy, Health, Well-Being, Passion...etc. These and all the chapters in the book relate to what everyone goes through in life. The material is a direct reflection of my Spiritual growth/self-realization and consists of insights that I have learned along the way from my personal experiences. My personal struggles have not only fueled the fire for my success but also my desire/goal to uplift as many people as possible so they can go after their goals and dreams, in turn bringing themselves out of hardship.

Coming Out of the Illusion: Realizing the Real You explores

themes of self-discovery and breaking through the illusions of societal conditioning. What inspired you to write this book, and what message do you hope readers will take away from it?

I was inspired to write the book because of suffering, lies and Illusion. Which stemmed from an increasingly warped society in which we live in and from a personal standpoint, trying to deal with everything. I want people to understand that no matter how terrible life seems to be at any-given-moment, you can break-free out of the Illusion and elevate yourself to new heights with consistent self-growth and perseverance. All you need is the truth and the proper tools in the form of whatever works best for you according to what you are

> Christopher Link, author and spiritual teacher, illuminates the path to enlightenment with wisdom born from personal transformation.

interested in.

You mention experiencing a spiritual awakening that led to the creation of your first book. Can you elaborate on what that awakening was like for you and how it transformed your perspective on life and spirituality?

My personal Spiritual awakening brought me out of the path of negative self-destruction/sabotage. - That was so bad, I was on the brink of suicide right before it happened. From the moment of my awakening, the light came back in my eyes, and I started on a new path to get my act together. The new perspective I had comes in the form of me being a value creator instead of a lost victim. I started

major self-introspection to figure out who I was and what I wanted to do with my new spiritually inspired life.

In your book, you discuss the search for something more and the quest for true reality. How do you define true reality, and what practices or insights do you suggest for individuals seeking to awaken to their own truth?

The Something More that we are all looking for has to do with life on another level of spiritual advancement. A knowing that a higher purpose/experience must be available besides the mundane existence of duality and ego-driven life, steeped in primitive low vibrations/mentality that is the third dimension. True reality is authentic life, beauty, love, compassion, joy, positive life construction...etc. -It is not aging/death - suffering/strife - negativity/destruction - hate/fear...etc. If individuals want to awaken to their own truth, then the answer is always to seek higher consciousness/ higher vibrations which leads to higher self-awareness.

Your journey includes a shift from a career in the flooring industry to becoming a spiritual author and teacher. Can you share more about how you navigated this transition and what challenges or revelations you encountered along the way?

I have been in the Flooring Business for 27 years now, up to present and still at it. I started to re-invent myself after my Spiritual Awakening in terms of self-education to prepare for a new career as a creative writer/author and Spiritual teacher. It has been a very long journey of perseverance and trying to navigate everything

by myself with very little support. I am still in transition mode with hopes to retire from the Flooring Business soon and focus 100% on being an author and Spiritual Life Coach. **As you continue on your path of service to others, what are your hopes and aspirations for the impact of your work, and how do you envision assisting people in their spiritual journeys moving forward?**

It is my goal/wish for all of my writing to reach as many people as possible who resonate with the material. I want to assist people with genuine, authentic, original, truth-filled and pure intention material, so they can experience better empowerment in their lives through spiritual enlightenment. Moving forward - Wait until you see and get a hold of book 2! I am working on finishing up book 2 now with hopes to release it in 2024! My second book is going to represent another level of advanced spiritual teaching and it also represents my level of spiritual growth. It will further assist people with the transitioning times as Earth has moved out of the third dimension. We are now navigating the early fourth dimension and quickly moving to the fifth. My other writings are in the form of a book - blog site entitled: My Golden Nuggets of Wisdom: Visionary Spirituality and I also have a Substack Newsletter with all original articles that is not related to the book material but still has a spiritual base with self-realization teachings.

PHOTO: Dance of Words: Lynn Slaughter, author of compelling mysteries, draws inspiration from her diverse experiences and passionate storytelling.

PHOTO BY SHANNON L. WELLS

Unveiling the Creative Tapestry

LYNN SLAUGHTER

Exploring the Artistic Journey, Societal Influences, and Family Dynamics Shaping Lynn's Captivating Narratives

Lynn Slaughter shares insights on how her dance background and sociology inform her mystery novels, crafting strong characters, and fostering diversity in literature.

Meet Lynn Slaughter: a connoisseur of arts, chocolate, and her husband's culinary delights. From a distinguished career in dance to wielding the pen as a prolific author, Lynn's journey reflects a mosaic of experiences that breathe life into her captivating narratives.

Her transition from the graceful world of dance to the realm of pen and paper was marked by an MFA in Writing Popular Fiction, a pivotal step that unleashed her storytelling prowess. Lynn's repertoire spans from captivating young adult mysteries to an intricate adult mystery series, beginning with MISSED CUE.

In conversation with Reader's House Magazine, Lynn delves into the profound influences that shape her craft. Her sociological insights, honed through immersion in diverse communities, infuse her narratives with a keen awareness of societal complexities. Themes of identity, family dynamics, and the pursuit of passion resonate deeply, reflecting her own journey of self-discovery and empowerment.

Lynn's characters, particularly her strong female protagonists, navigate through the labyrinth of challenges, drawing strength from their vulnerabilities and triumphing against adversities. Their journeys, intricately crafted against the backdrop of suspenseful plots and compelling mysteries, mirror the resilience and tenacity that define Lynn's own narrative arc.

As a grandmother to five cherished souls, Lynn finds inspiration in the innocence and wonder of youth. Her commitment to diversity in literature, fueled by the enriching bond with her African American grandson, underscores her belief in the transformative power of representation.

Join us as Lynn Slaughter unravels the threads of her storytelling tapestry, offering insights into her creative process, the resonance of her personal experiences, and the enduring power of literature to inspire and empower.

Your background in sociology and as a professional dancer and dance educator seems to have influenced the themes and characters in your novels. How do your experiences in these fields shape the stories you write, particularly in books like _LEISHA'S SONG, WHILE I DANCED, AND MISSED CUE_?

I not only majored in sociology but had the opportunity to live and work in an African American community during the summer when I was in college. This was a

life-changing experience for me and made me extremely aware of my own white privilege and how complicated it was to be a person of color in a society where discrimination is baked into every institution. My summer roommate was an aspiring opera singer with a voice from God. I loved her very much, and in many ways, she inspired my protagonist in *LEISHA'S SONG*.

As for my background as a professional dancer and dance educator, I think it led to authenticity in the dance scenes in *WHILE I DANCED* and *MISSED CUE*. Living that life gave me insight into what it's like to be passionate about an art form which is very competitive while also lending itself to close friendships and romances. Dancers spend long hours together in the studio and on stage. I don't think it's an accident that I met my husband in a dance company!

Many of your novels feature strong female protagonists facing complex challenges and navigating intricate relationships. What inspires you to center your stories around such characters, and how do you approach crafting their journeys and development?

Well, obviously, I am female, and I think growing up can be a complicated journey for women. We're often raised to please and to be caring and sensitive to the needs and feelings of others. What sometimes gets lost is the need to balance caring for others with the need to honor our own needs and interests.

In my writing process, I often start out with a wisp of an idea, often drawn from something I've witnessed or heard about. For example, an adult dance student once shared with me that during high school, her twin had been murdered. Her story stuck with me and became the premise for *IT SHOULD HAVE BEEN YOU*.

Before doing any plotting, I delve into character, especially their backstories. In Clara's case, she grew up in a family of musicians, and her murdered twin had been a piano prodigy. Clara's

gift was writing, not music. In her family, her sister got most of the attention, and she was more or less the forgotten child. Her emotional journey had to do with recognizing her own worth.

Your bio mentions that you returned to school to earn your MFA in Writing Popular Fiction. How did this decision impact your writing career, and what valuable lessons did you learn during your studies that you apply to your writing process today?

I benefited greatly from my

MFA program. I learned to meet deadlines, and I not only received constructive feedback from my mentors but lots of encouragement and support. Perhaps the best lesson I learned is that you have to put your "butt-in-the chair" on a regular basis to make progress as a writer.

In *Deadly Setup* and *It Should Have Been You*, your characters find themselves embroiled in murder mysteries and legal battles. What drew you to the mystery genre, and how do you approach creating suspenseful plots and compelling whodunits?

I blame it all on all those Nancy Drew mysteries I gobbled up as a child! I love the idea of a proactive young woman determined to solve a mystery and restore justice.

In plotting, I try to present a protagonist with lots of obstacles and red herrings. It can't be too easy, or it's boring. And of course, the stakes for the protagonist have to continue to rise until either their life, or life as they have known it, is in grave danger.

Family dynamics and the quest for identity seem to be recurring themes in your novels, such as in *Leisha's Song* and *While I Danced.* How do you explore these themes through your characters' experiences, and what messages or insights do you hope readers take away from your stories?

I grew up with an autocratic father who laid out life scripts for

his three daughters. Our interests, passions, and dreams were largely discounted. This was a painful experience, and there's no question it has influenced the themes in my writing. In both *LEISHA'S SONG* and *WHILE I DANCED*, parental figures actively discourage their daughters from pursuing their artistic passions. I hope that what readers will take away from their stories is that coming of age involves the difficult process of learning to stand up for yourself and make choices for your own life, as well as the value of creating your own intentional family.

Your bio also mentions your role as a grandmother of five. How does your family life and the relationships you have with your grandchildren influence your writing, if at all?

I love reading with my grandchildren, and it's made me so aware of the joy and meaning books add to our lives. My close relationship with my eldest grandson, who is African American, has also been a powerful reminder that young people of color need lots more books with people who look like them. In addition, one of my younger grandsons read a draft of my forthcoming middle grade novel, *THE BIG SWITCH: VARNEY AND CEDRIC*. His enthusiasm about the story encouraged me to persevere in finding a publisher.

Introducing
LIZ ALTERMAN
Navigating the Roller Coaster of Unemployment with Humour and Heart

Liz Alterman discusses the inspiration behind "Sad Sacked," balancing comedy with serious themes, personal anecdotes, crafting suspense, and societal pressures in unemployment.

In a recent interview with Reader's House Magazine, Alterman sheds light on the inspiration behind "Sad Sacked," a poignant memoir delving into the challenges faced by families grappling with sudden job loss. Drawing from her own personal journey alongside her husband, Alterman offers a refreshingly honest narrative that navigates the tumultuous terrain of unemployment with humour and resilience.

At the heart of "Sad Sacked" lies a quest for authenticity amidst societal pressures to maintain appearances. Alterman candidly shares anecdotes that weave through the fabric of her storytelling, offering readers a glimpse into the raw emotions and absurdities that accompany the pursuit of livelihood in an unpredictable world.

With a deft hand, Alterman balances the comedic elements of her narrative with the weight of its underlying themes, crafting a tapestry of laughter and introspection. She seamlessly intertwines personal experiences with societal expectations, resonating deeply with readers navigating similar suburban landscapes.

Readers of Alterman's previous work, such as The Perfect Neighbourhood, recognize her prowess in crafting suspenseful tales that grip the imagination. In the interview, Alterman provides insights into her approach to building tension and weaving unexpected twists, inviting readers on an exhilarating journey through the corridors of her narratives.

As Alterman candidly reflects on her writing process, she acknowledges the invaluable support of her family and fellow writers, underscoring the collaborative spirit that infuses her creative endeavours.

In Sad Sacked and beyond, Liz Alterman emerges as a beacon of resilience, reminding readers that even in the face of adversity, laughter and camaraderie can light the path forward. Through her words, she invites us to embrace the complexities of the human experience with empathy and humour, forging connections that transcend the pages of her books.

What inspired you to write Sad Sacked and delve into the challenges faced by families dealing with sudden unemployment?

When my husband and I lost our jobs within six weeks of one another, we were in a state of shock and spent a lot of time asking, "How did we get here?"

We were in our forties, so we definitely couldn't afford to retire. (Who can these days?)

As we embarked on our job hunt, I found plenty of content designed to help you spruce up your resume, craft your cover letter, and nail an interview, but I didn't see much that honestly addressed the mental and emotional toll unemployment takes on you.

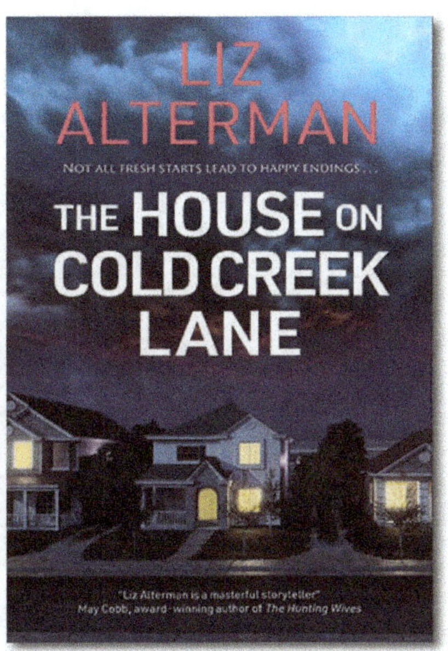

Dive into a world of suspense, laughter, and heart with Liz Alterman's captivating trio:
'The Perfect Neighborhood,' 'Sad Sacked' and 'The House on Cold Creek Lane.'

Liz Alterman's candid narrative in "Sad Sacked" navigates unemployment with humor and authenticity, resonating deeply with readers' experiences.

I wanted to read something that brought a bit of humor to the absurdity of it all—from the shock of discovering that companies had replaced health care benefits with bagel breakfasts to spotting a great opening on LinkedIn and realizing that though it was posted only 20 minutes earlier, 400 people had already applied.

I longed to hear someone say, "I lost my job and I'm up at 2 a.m. attempting to DoorDash a McFlurry to calm my nerves."

In the book, I explore how unemployment is one of those things that you can't fully grasp until you've lived through it. I also wanted to remove the shame that often comes with job loss because, really, it can happen to any of us at any time.

Can you share any personal experiences or anecdotes that influenced the storyline or characters in your book?

Absolutely! When I'd been out of work for about six months, I spotted an opening for a digital editor position at a major Manhattan museum. My neighbor just happened to work there so I asked if he'd put in a good word for me. He did, and weeks later I had an interview scheduled.

It took me about ninety minutes by car to get there. When I finally arrived, the interviewer had forgotten our appointment. Luckily, she was in the building so we went ahead with the interview, but it was after lunch and she could barely keep her eyes open. It slowly dawned on me that she'd only brought me in as a favor to my neighbor. By the time I raced back to my car before my meter expired, I was ready to beat the dashboard with my bone-crushing heels in frustration.

Getting our hopes up only to be let down felt like a recurring theme in our unemployment journey. I knew there had to be other people on this roller coaster. I wanted to tell our story in the spirit of "misery shared is misery halved."

How do you balance the comedic elements with the serious themes of pressure and resilience in your writing?

I often say humor is my drug of choice. Growing up, my mom routinely quoted Erma Bombeck, and this line really resonates with me, "If you can't make it better, you can laugh at it."

Similarly, Nora Ephron has this great bit of wisdom: "When you slip on a banana peel, people laugh at you. But when you tell people you slipped on a banana peel, it's your laugh."

I try to embrace these philosophies in my life and my writing.

In Sad Sacked, you explore societal expectations and the pressure to maintain appearances. How do you think this resonates with readers, particularly those in similar suburban settings?

When you live in an affluent suburb, there's an expectation that you'll maintain a certain lifestyle. And yet a lot of people face financial (and other) challenges. The pressure to keep up can be exhausting and almost paralyzing.

Once I began confiding in friends and neighbors about our job losses, I was surprised by how many had gone through something similar. I hope that people who read Sad Sacked and have experienced unexpected unemployment feel less alone.

Your previous work, The Perfect Neighborhood, received praise for its suspenseful storytelling. How do you approach crafting tension and twists in your narratives?

I love to read thrillers and suspenseful stories—ones that you can't put down no matter what else you're supposed to be doing. I strive to provide that experience for readers. That said, I find it really challenging because, as the author, I know the ending. So I'm always worrying, "Is this too obvious?" or "Is this too obscure?" Striking that balance and trying to end chapters in ways that make readers say, "I know I should start dinner, but I'm just going to read one more chapter…" that's my ultimate goal.

I'm also very fortunate to have a supportive family and a wonderful fellow writer friend who will read rough drafts for me and let me know what's working and what's falling flat. I'd be lost without them.

KELLY ELIZABETH HUSTON

Navigating Genre, Empowering Characters, and Embracing the Indie Journey

Explore the multifaceted world of author Kelly Elizabeth Huston, as she discusses her eclectic storytelling, empowering female protagonists, and the transition to indie publishing in a captivating interview.

Kelly Elizabeth Huston, a luminary in the realm of fiction, crafts narratives that are as eclectic as they are captivating. Her stories traverse genres with ease, weaving together elements of humour, romance, suspense, and mystery into tapestries of literary delight. With an unmistakable knack for infusing her tales with heart, humour, and a touch of intrigue, Kelly's novels offer readers an immersive experience that lingers long after the final page is turned.

Venturing beyond the constraints of traditional publishing, Kelly embraced the indie route with gusto, propelling her lite-

Author Kelly Elizabeth Huston, weaving tales of humour, romance, and suspense with a touch of magic

rary creations into the world with fervour and determination. Her journey underscores a profound belief in the power of storytelling and the autonomy of the artist—a sentiment that resonates deeply in every word she writes.

In her latest interview with Reader's House magazine, Kelly Eliza-beth Huston opens up about her creative process, the inspiration behind her novels, and the challenges and rewards of her transition to indie publishing. Through insightful discussions on themes of resilience, empowerment, and the intricacies of the human experience, Kelly offers readers a glimpse into the inner workings of her imagination.

With strong, multifaceted female protagonists at the helm of her narratives, Kelly champions the importance of agency and diversity in storytelling. Her characters are a reflection of the comp-lexities of real life, navigating challenges with wit, determination, and an unwavering spirit.

From the whimsical to the profound, Kelly's novels strike a delicate balance between levity and depth, infusing even the most suspenseful moments with a dash of humour. Her dedication to entertaining her readers shines through in every chapter, inviting them on a journey filled with laughter, tears, and everything in between.

Aspiring writers seeking guidance will find solace in Kelly's advice, rooted in her own experiences as a pantser—a testament to the beauty of embracing one's unique creative process. Through her words of wisdom, Kelly encourages fellow storytellers to follow their instincts, embrace the joy of creation, and fearlessly chart their own path in the world of literature.

In essence, Kelly Elizabeth Huston's interview offers a glimpse into the mind of a visionary storyteller—one whose passion for her craft illuminates every page, leaving an indelible mark on the literary landscape. Join us as we delve into the rich tapestry of Kelly's imagination and discover the magic woven within her words.

Your novels seem to blend different genres seamlessly, offering readers a mix of hu-

Enter a world where humor meets heart, and suspense dances with romance. Discover the magic within Kelly Elizabeth Huston's captivating novels.

mour, romance, suspense, and mystery. What draws you to this eclectic style of storytelling, and how do you manage to balance these elements effectively?

It's a blessing and a curse. I suppose I fell for the old adage: Write the book you want to read. Not the best marketing move for the traditional space, but I'm finding readers who enjoy the genre blend. Life is funny and scary and romantic and sad, so I enjoy books that mirror that. I haven't had many complaints. Most readers want characters to root for. Give them that and they will follow them anywhere.

Tex Miller Is Dead explores the intricate relationship between an author and her fictional creation, Tex Miller. What inspired you to delve into this metafictional concept, and how did you navigate the complexities of blurring the lines between reality and fiction within the narrative?

Sometimes, as writers, we reach a moment when we think, "I'd like to see other people." My first complete manuscript, that lives in a drawer and will NEVER see the light of day, consumed me, but I wanted to try something different. Still, I didn't know how to let go of the characters in that first story. That's how the notion of "killing" a protagonist developed. How do you evict characters and stories that live inside your head? TEX and his fun just tumbled out of me from there.

In A Very Crowded House, the protagonist Jocelyn Durand finds herself facing unexpected challenges when she meets her literary idol, Asher Cray. Can you discuss the themes of idolization, perception versus reality, and overcoming obstacles that are

explored in this novel?

I touch on this idea of literary idols in TEX MILLER too. I have a few idols but I cannot imagine meeting them. Don't really want to, but my hope is, just like Callie and Asher and Jocelyn... my idols are just regular people, with the same fears, quirks, insecurities as the rest of us.

A Girl, Stuck" introduces us to Harriet "Harry" Smith, a private investigator with a complicated past. What motivated you to create such a multifaceted character, and how does Harry's journey reflect broader themes of resilience, redemption, and moral ambiguity?

I love Harry so much. She is incredibly flawed but in the way I think so many of us are in those early adult years—so sure of who we are and what we can accomplish, but not realizing all the study, effort, and falling flat it takes to truly be prepared to succeed. We want to skip the hard part, the grunt work. Throw forbidden romantic attraction on that fire and even the best and brightest are going to make some serious mistakes. Again, the reflection of real life. It's how one perseveres in the face of all that tumult that makes an interesting story.

Many of your novels feature strong female protagonists navigating complex situations. How important is it for you to portray empowered women in your stories, and what messages do you hope readers take away from these characters?

Well, I hope they end up stronger in the end, for sure. "My" women are sorts of things: smart, generous, wicked, not the brightest bulb, funny, fierce advocates, and troubling antagonists. I could go on. Whether they are

a side character or the principal attraction, I hope the women I create are as varied as in real life. Agency is the key. If they don't have it, they need to claim it or suffer the consequences. Hopefully, good thwarts bad. Eventually.

As someone who has transitioned from traditional publishing to indie publishing, what have been the most significant challenges and rewards of this journey?

How does being an indie author influence your creative process and interaction with your readership? The learning curve is steep. I was determined to make the leap from traditional to self-publishing with as little difference in end-product as possible. It means a significant investment in time and money. That said, I wouldn't change a thing. In the same time (two years) one traditionally published writer-friend will get her book to market I will have ended my relationship with my agent and published four books. And for me, nothing is better than getting read and enjoyed by strangers. Add the control I have over design and content, not having to share royalties, or face voided contracts? In the absence of some extraordinary lightning strike, I believe the indie route is the best track for my books over the slow-motion, gatekept, traditional publishing model. No matter the artform, I believe the creators should always end up on top.

Your novels often incorporate elements of humour, even in the midst of suspenseful or emotional scenes. How do you approach incorporating humour into your writing, and why do you believe it's essential to maintain a balance of levity in your stories?

I grew up with Reader's Digest

and their "Laughter is the Best Medicine" segments. I am a believer and I live my life that way. If I'm hurt or scared or nervous, embarrassed, excited, surprised... you name it, I tend to lead with the funny. Not always appropriate, but that's me. My goal with my writing has always been to entertain. Sure, I hope readers think and feel and open their minds to how others might think and feel like so many stories my more serious novelist-friends write, but in the end I hope I have satisfied the reader and they think, "Wow, that was fun!"

Can you provide insight into your writing process? Do you meticulously plan out your plots and characters, or do you allow the story to evolve more organically as you write?

Additionally, what advice do you have for aspiring writers looking to embark on their own writing journey? I am a complete and total PANTSER. I have tried plotting —taken workshops, read craft books, but my brain doesn't work that way. I'll "meet" a character and see a scene, then try to find my way to that place. That scene has NEVER turned out to be what I thought it was at first. Not once. It fascinates me how I am so wrong every time. I am a big believer in doing whatever works for the creative. Whatever brings the joy... and the words to the page.

An Exclusive Interview with
ASHTON AUGUST
From Mindset to Philanthropy, Exploring the Journey of a Wellness and Advocate

Explore Ashton August's journey from writing to wellness entrepreneurship. Discover her insights on mindset, self-motivation, social impact, and van-life adventures

Meet Ashton August, a dynamic force in the realm of wellness, whose passion for fostering positive change transcends boundaries. With a diverse background encompassing writing, yoga instruction, entrepreneurship, and philanthropy, Ashton embodies a holistic approach to life that resonates deeply with her audience. As a wellness expert and the author of two motivational books, *Learn Grow Shift* and *A Year of Self-Motivation for Women*, with her third book, *Mindfulness Practices for Anxiety*, on the horizon, Ashton's journey is a testament to the power of self-discovery and personal growth.

Grounded in her experience as a Creative Nonfiction Writing MFA graduate and a seasoned yoga instructor for over 13 years, Ashton's mission took shape with the inception of YouAligned.com, a leading wellness website, and YA Classes, a mission-driven yoga, meditation, and fitness app. Through these platforms, Ashton has touched the lives of millions worldwide, providing invaluable resources and guidance for mind-body-life wellness.

In our exclusive interview with Ashton, we delve into the motivations driving her multifaceted endeavors and the impact she envisions for the wellness community. From her insights on fostering positive self-talk and mindset to her unwavering commitment to social impact, Ashton's wisdom shines through as she shares personal anecdotes and strategies for maintaining balance amidst her various roles.

As a motivational speaker, Ashton's messages of mindset wellness and the importance of holistic well-being resonate deeply in an era marked by constant change and challenges. With a keen emphasis on the intersection of mindset and wellness, she champions the transformative power of self-care and intentional living.

Beyond her professional endeavors, Ashton's adventurous spirit finds expression in her van-life journey, where she, alongside her husband and rescue dogs, embarks on a transformative odyssey across the country. Through these experiences, Ashton discovers

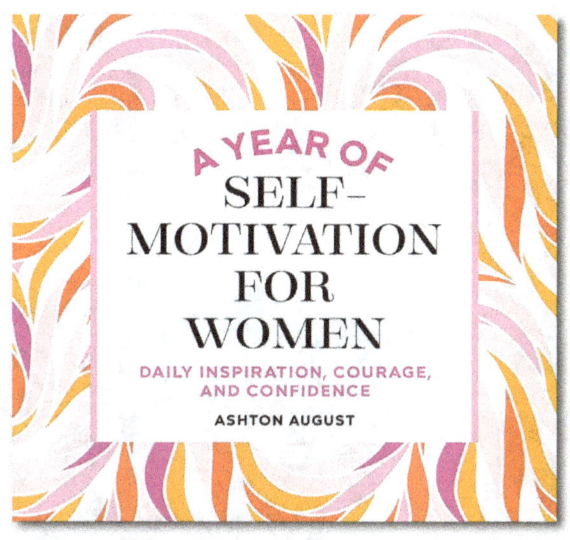

invaluable lessons in flexibility, gratitude, and the beauty of embracing the unknown.

Join us as we uncover the inspiring journey of Ashton August, a trailblazer whose dedication to empowering others and making a meaningful impact continues to illuminate pathways to wellness and personal fulfillment.

What inspired you to create YouAligned.com and YA Classes, and how do you see these platforms impacting the wellness community?

Shortly after receiving my MFA in Creative NonFiction Writing and becoming an English Professor, I also started teaching yoga. I wanted to bridge my passion for writing with my love of yoga and desire to spread wellness on a global level. This was when YogiApproved (we've since rebranded to YouAligned) was born in 2015.

YouAligned.com is our yoga and wellness online magazine with thousands of free articles on yoga, meditation, mindfulness, nutrition and more resources for mind-body-life wellness. We are named Top Ten Global Yoga Resources with over a million annual readers! YA Classes is our 5-star yoga and fitness membership app. Between our website, app, and YouTube, we have had the immense privilege of spreading wellness to millions of people around the world.

Your book A Year of Self-Motivation for Women focuses on fostering positive self-talk and

mindset. Can you share a personal experience or anecdote that inspired this book's creation?

I have always been a high achiever, but for most of my life it came from a place of trying to prove myself. Once I flipped that script from striving for approval to accepting and loving myself as I am, I started exploring the power of my self-talk. I realized that I still had that old narrative replaying in my head of "never good enough, not worthy, etc."

A healthy mindset and empowering self-talk opens the door to an abundantly fulfilling life. Tapping into this power motivated me to share it with others, particularly women. Because as women, society holds us to often unrealistic expectations that, when gone unchecked can destroy our sense of self-worth. And without self-worth, how can we expect to have an empowered mindset and the motivation that comes with it?

As a motivational speaker, what are some common themes or messages you find yourself emphasizing in your talks, and why are they important to you?

My two dominant themes are mindset and wellness. Often I blend the two for what I like to call mindset wellness which blends emotional intelligence (EQ), empowering self-talk, and wellness practices for a fortified mindset.

Mindset is everything, and self-talk dictates our entire lives, from the actions we take to the decisions we make.

Wellness is key to success. Wellness encompasses an active lifestyle, nutrition + hydration, work-life balance, and mental / emotional / spiritual fulfillment. Speaking from experience, if you don't shore up your energy supply with consistent and intentional self-care and work-life balance, you will

experience burn out. The secret to ultimate productivity is what we do when we are not working.

How do you balance your roles as an entrepreneur, author, yoga instructor, and speaker? Do you have any specific strategies or rituals that help you stay focused and productive?

While I do have this significantly dialed in, it's still a work in progress. That said, here are my keys for maintaining my sanity, motivation, and passion for all that I do so I can continue to show up and give my best:

1. My morning routine of hydration, meditation, and intention to start my day

2. Rest for ultimate success! It took me years to get to this point, but I take 1-2 full days off each week as a non-negotiable.

3. Daily exercise for my physical + mental health

4. Commitment to self-care and non-work activities that nourish my soul and my creativity: reading, spending time outdoors, hot baths, time with friends

5. Eat the Frog: complete the biggest task on the list first

6. 4 hours of deep focused work instead of 8 hours of distracted, hectic 'multitasking'

5. Your commitment to social impact, such as planting food-producing trees for farming communities in West Africa through YA Classes, is admirable. What led you to incorporate such initiatives into your business model, and what impact have you seen so far?

Thank you for this accolade! I believe altruism should be a key

pillar of every business, and it certainly is for mine. When we first created YA Classes, we wanted to find a way to motivate our members to stay consistent with their yoga. More importantly, we wanted to find a way to give back, and that's when the idea to quantify classes with tree planting was born. 312,000+ trees planted later, we couldn't be more proud of the impact this has had for our members, the planet, and for the farming communities in Sub-Saharan Africa where these trees are planted.

6. Van-life seems like an adventurous lifestyle choice. How has traveling around the country with your husband and rescue dogs influenced your work and personal growth, if at all?

Like any form of travel, van life can be intense, stressful, and full of unknowns and this has taught me a lot about myself. It has opened me up to personal growth in ways I never expected, from deepening my self-reliance and trust that everything will work out, to helping me with my patience and ability to go with the flow instead of trying to control everything.

As an entrepreneur, van life has taught me flexibility, discipline, and immense gratitude for the life I've built that I'm able to travel and work remotely. As an author, nothing is more inspiring than being on the open road! Travel in all forms has influenced my writing and deepened my prowess as a writer.

PHOTO: *Susan Mac Nicol, celebrated romance author and screenwriter, in a candid moment.*

Exploring Love and London

SUSAN MAC NICOL

Behind the Scenes with the Prolific Romance Author

Susan Mac Nicol is a name that romance readers hold dear, known for her ability to weave steamy, sexy, and fun contemporary romance stories. With a knack for suspenseful, gritty, and dark themes, her work remains consistently entertaining. Beyond her role as a prolific author, Susan is the Editor in Chief at Divine Magazine, an online entertainment e-zine, and holds memberships with both The Society of Authors and the Authors Guild in the US. Her talents extend into screenwriting, where she has earned accolades for scripts based on her own published works.

In our exclusive interview, Susan delves into the inspiration behind her beloved Men of London series, which brings the vibrant city of

Susan Mac Nicol discusses her inspiration for the Men of London series, the influence of Benedict Cumberbatch on her writing, and her experiences in both novel and scriptwriting.

London to life through diverse and captivating stories. She shares her journey of transforming admiration for Benedict Cumberbatch into the character Bennett Saville in *Cassandra by Starlight*, offering insight into the challenges and triumphs of adapting a story from screenplay to novel. Furthermore, Susan opens up about exploring the quirky and intriguing world of London's fetish community in *Welcome to Fetish Alley*, ensuring authenticity and sensitivity in her depiction of this unique subculture.

We also discuss how her award-winning scriptwriting experience influences her novel writing,

especially in terms of dialogue, pacing, and visual storytelling. Susan's versatility spans across genres, blending contemporary romance with elements of romantasy, suspense, and emotional depth. She reflects on balancing these diverse elements to create stories that resonate deeply with readers.

Finally, Susan's love for theatre, live music concerts, and horror films serves as a wellspring of inspiration for her storytelling and creative process. From the grandeur of *Phantom of the Opera* to the psychological thrill of Stephen King's *The Stand,* her wide-ranging interests continually fuel her

creative spirit.

Join us as Susan Mac Nicol takes us on a journey through her literary and personal adventures, offering a glimpse into the passions and experiences that shape her writing.

Your Men of London series features diverse and captivating stories set in the vibrant landscape of London. What inspired you to create this series, and how do you approach crafting the unique tales for each instalment?

I'm a lover of London and I thought it would be wonderful to create stories based around London and introduce the readers to the vibrant city I love. It has so much to offer, and by seeing the city through the eyes of these different men as they look for love and a relationship, I believed it would create a world

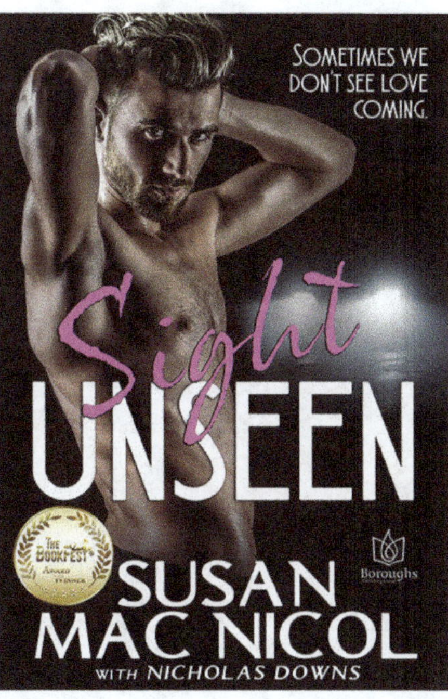

A selection of Susan Mac Nicol's beloved novels, showcasing her diverse range and captivating storytelling.

Susan Mac Nicol captivates readers with her dynamic storytelling, creating unforgettable characters and richly detailed worlds that resonate deeply.

for people to escape into, especially as my reading audience tends to be people in the US. I wanted them to go on an adventure with me to see this part of the world. I've been to every place I use in the book, including - ahem - Hampstead Heath where I believe Mr Cumberbatch swims in the heath ponds. No ulterior motive there then... :)

Cassandra by Starlight was inspired by your admiration for Benedict Cumberbatch. How did your fascination with him influence the creation of the character Bennett Saville, and what challenges did you encounter in adapting the story from screenplay to novel?

Oh there's such a story behind the creation of this novel. I am obsessed with the man to the point that my readers and friends send me anything they find about him, knowing I'll love it no matter what. I was so keen on him that I decided I wanted one of my own. The only way to do this was to write a novel where he, (aka Bennett Saville) featured in his own story. I modelled Cassandra on me (being a woman ten years older) and then I could express my fantasies and desires in the story using Cassie as an unwitting alter ego. It was wonderful. When the opportunity came to write a pilot episode for a film festival, I did so and won the award. It was the first time I've ever done any screen writing and it was a learning curve. As a novelist I tend to be rather wordy, so condensing my words into short, pithy screen writing proved much a challenge. I was told that if I could get my screenplay green lighted, Benedict's casting agent (who I was in touch with at the time) would see if the divine Mr Cumberbatch fancied the role, because he was wanting to do something romantic! I was even on a local radio station with another Cumberbatch loving presenter, while we discussed everything Benedict.

Welcome to Fetish Alley introduces readers to the quirky and intriguing world of London's fetish community. What drew you to explore this setting, and how did you ensure authenticity and sensitivity in depicting this subculture in your writing?

I am very fortunate to have met many wonderful people in my time writing gay romance, or as we call it, Male/Male romance. My connections with some of these individuals allowed me to do the research (as some of them are in the BDSM and fetish scene) and find the best ways to portray the characters to their very best. This series is less about the Fetish scene and more about the writing of detective stories and romance set in a backdrop of a very special fetish club and with some rather unique appetites. It was huge fun learning about this world and I do hope I represented it with respect and sensitivity. One of my books, Saving Alexander, which features BDSM, is actually recommended by a therapist in the US as a book to read and understand the torment of a traumatic past and abuse.

As an award-winning scriptwriter, how does your experience in scriptwriting inform your approach to writing novels, particularly in terms of dialogue, pacing, and visual storytelling?

My editor has a way of bringing me down to earth when she rings me up and tells me, "Sue, you aren't being paid by the word for your books, so less wordy, more show and tell, please." Script writing gives you this discipline to say something that in a novel may be a scene, but yet in a screenplay is merely a sentence. Of course, the positive side is you have the film director's and the actors vision of how the scene will play out, so this alleviate the writer from too much exposition and description. Dialogue is also one of my favourite things to write, so script writing allows me to release that energy I have for my characters to verbally communicate.

Your writing spans genres from contemporary romance to romantasy, with elements of suspense, grit, and darkness woven throughout. How do you balance these diverse elements to create stories that are both entertaining and emotionally resonant for readers?

I'm a huge reader and I read a variety of genres, from MM romances, to Urban fantasy, to dystopian novels and anything else that takes my fancy. The diversity I see in these stories brings me a solid grounding in the genre to develop the knowledge to create my own worlds and characters with a different twist. I'm a BIG believer in research for my next series called Monarchs of Magic, so I went to Scotland to scope out the valley the book is set in, and spoke to some wonderful Highland locals about their experiences. I'm also very much into realism, and love to factor in real life emotions and experiences into my books. I think this is what makes my stories resonate because people can identify with the experiences and the characters.

In addition to writing, you're also a fan of theatre, live music concerts, and horror films. How do these interests influence your storytelling and creative process, and do you draw inspiration from specific experiences or moments in these activities?

The best show I ever saw in London was Phantom of the Opera - three times. The sheer magnificence of the music, the captivating lyrics, and the incredible storytelling made me want to create something similar. I may not have done an Andrew Lloyd Webber, but I do think I've created worlds and people within them that people love to read about and identify with. I'm a very visual person, so watching live acts on stage and theatre really stimulates my creative spirit and the muse becomes animated and tells me to get the hell to work. As for horror books, my favourite writer is Stephen King and his novel The Stand was the benchmark against which I compared every horror novel I read thereafter. I adore horror films, but not slasher movies, only the real psychological terror invoking productions that make you sit on the end of your seat, and which have a chilling finale.

Available in
PRINT

Americas to Australia Europe to Africa Reader's House is available over 190 countries and thousands of retaiers, platforms including Amazon, Barnes & Noble, Walmart, Waterstone's .....

ELECTRONIC

It is an electronic (flip book) format and interactive. Accessable from electronic devices like pc, smart phone, notepads..

ONLINE

All interviews, we conduct make them accessable online for free.

SOCIAL MEDIA

We are on Facebook, Instagram and X. Please follow us on social media @readershousemag

contact us today for an interview opportunity at
editor@readershouse.co.uk

Subscribe Now!

YES! I would like a subscription to

☐ Current Issue for   ☐ Includes Shipping and Handling

☐ One-Year Subscription (_______ Issues) for

☐ Two-Year Subscription (_______ Issues) for

☐ I am a renewing a current subscription   ☐ I am a new subscriber

Name: _________________________________ Phone: _______________

Shipping Address: ____

Billing Address: ____

Email: ____

☐ Yes, I would like to receive updates, newsletters and special offers
☐ No, I would NOT like to receive updates, newsletters and special offers

Payment Type: ☐ Cash   ☐ Check

Please mail this form to:
Magazine Name: *Reader's House* by Newyox 200 Suite, 134-146 Curtain Road EC2A 3AR London   readershouse.co.uk

www.ingramcontent.com/pod-product-compliance
Lightning Source LLC
Chambersburg PA
CBHW081330090726
47907CB00010B/2432